She couldn't stop thinking about him

Suddenly, as if from nowhere, a familiar voice said, "Hello, Sunshine, I've been waiting for you to show up."

Caitlin whirled around and found Bryce smiling at her. Speechlessly, she stared at him.

"I'm the reason for your journey, remember?" he teased.

"I'm here on business," she said, regaining composure. "You're just the first of a series of articles."

"Just?"

His smugness annoyed her. "I decided to start with the small fry," she informed him tartly.

"Liar," he laughed. "I told you once you were gorgeous enough to be a 'Slattery' girl, but I want you to be my girl alone."

"No thanks. I'm here to work," Caitlin said briskly.

"You're here because I arranged a deal with your editor. I get you in return for the lowdown on my future. A world exclusive."

WELCOME
TO THE WONDERFUL WORLD
OF *Harlequin Presents*

Interesting, informative and entertaining,
each Harlequin romance portrays an appealing
and original love story. With a varied array
of settings, we may lure you on an African safari,
to a quaint Welsh village, or an exotic Riviera
location—anywhere and everywhere that adventurous
men and women fall in love.

As publishers of Harlequin romances, we're
extremely proud of our books. Since 1949,
Harlequin Enterprises has built its publishing
reputation on the solid base of quality and
originality. Our stories are the most popular
paperback romances sold in North America; every
month, eight new titles are released and sold at
nearly every book-selling store in Canada and the
United States.

A free catalog listing all available Harlequin romances
can be yours by writing to the

HARLEQUIN READER SERVICE
1440 South Priest Drive, Tempe, AZ 85281
Canadian address: Stratford, Ontario N5A 6W2

We sincerely hope you enjoy reading
this Harlequin Presents.

Yours truly,

THE PUBLISHERS

ELIZABETH OLDFIELD

dream hero

Harlequin Books

TORONTO • NEW YORK • LOS ANGELES • LONDON
AMSTERDAM • PARIS • SYDNEY • HAMBURG
STOCKHOLM • ATHENS • TOKYO • MILAN

Harlequin Presents first edition June 1983
ISBN 0-373-10604-1

Original hardcover edition published in 1983
by Mills & Boon Limited

Printed in U.S.A.

CHAPTER ONE

MATTHEW disappeared ahead into the swirl of passengers. For a minute or two Caitlin struggled to keep pace with his rapid strides, then she gave a rueful pout and halted, shrugging the pale fur jacket closer around her shoulders. She switched the bulging holdall to the other hand and, sighing, set off again after him. The platform was crowded. People rushed here and there, shepherding tardy children, heaving luggage, scanning the carriage windows for empty seats.

Matthew was waiting. 'There's room in here.'

Caitlin stepped before him into the train and gave a smile of gratitude as he swung the large suitcase on to the rack above her head and reached for a canvas tote bag.

'Are you sure you can cope?' he asked, jamming the bag firmly into position. 'Grab a porter at Derby. Take a taxi. Don't try to struggle on the bus with all this luggage.' His grey eyes swept anxiously over the rack, the girl and the leather holdall.

'Don't fret,' she chided with a smile. 'I'm perfectly capable of looking after myself.' She patted the seat beside her. 'For heaven's sake, sit down and catch your breath. There's still five minutes before the train departs.'

Matthew sank down, pushing back the fall of fair hair from his brow. 'Have you everything you need—fruit, chocolates, something to read?'

'Yes, sir,' she teased, her hazel eyes sparkling. '*And* I'll ring you as soon as I arrive, *and* I won't talk to any strange men.'

He laughed. 'Especially that, avoid them like the

plague.' He glanced at her lovingly. Strange men were an occupational hazard as far as Caitlin was concerned. Her slender figure, oval face with its high cheekbones, and torrent of chestnut-coloured hair attracted men like flies. But she was his—well, nearly his, he adjusted mentally. A frown creased his brow. 'I still feel it's a damned cheek, Joelle expecting you to care for her father during his convalescence. It's her duty. You're only his niece.'

A soothing hand rested on the rough tweed of his sleeve.

'We've been through all this before. Joelle can't leave London. There's an audition for a new musical, and it's vital she's there. It could be her big break.'

'Big break!' The words spluttered out in disgust. 'Every audition is supposed to be her so-called "big break", but what has she achieved so far—three small stage parts and five minutes as a television corpse!' He gave a sarcastic snort. 'Odd days sprawled half naked over car bonnets at motor shows, or passing round caviar at designer jeans promotions, don't count as acting.'

Caitlin fingered the lapel of her mulberry-coloured trouser suit. 'I'm looking forward to staying with Uncle Desmond.' There was a warning bite of determination in her tone. 'I need a break from the rat race. I need time to think.' Their eyes collided warily and bounced apart. 'Besides, Joelle loathes the countryside. She's a city girl. Tarmacadam runs in her veins.'

'But I shan't see you for a whole month.' Sulkiness tainted the boyish good looks.

'Uncle Desmond suffered a stroke,' Caitlin said flatly, her patience beginning to wear thin. 'It takes time to recover from something like that. His wife died years ago, and I refuse to allow him to struggle back to good health alone.' Circles of hot colour flared in her cheeks. 'I have two weeks' holiday in hand, I've arranged an additional two of unpaid leave, and that's all there is to it.' Her full mouth tightened. 'I know the stroke was mild, thank goodness, and I know Uncle Desmond's home help, Mrs Richards, goes in regularly, and I know he won't come to any harm, but . . .' Her voice lifted on a note of agitation. 'But he'll still feel lonely in the evenings and at weekends.' She paused. 'And it will be a relief for me to get away from the magazine for a while.'

And from you.' The last phrase went unspoken, but they both heard it.

For months she had been stalling, adroitly avoiding any commitment to Matthew, but suddenly a decision was being forced on her. He was an accountant, a clever one, and had been offered a plum job as Head of Finance at the New York office of the international company in which he worked. It was a three-year appointment and he had no intention of turning it down. His future was developing along the lines he had planned. 'Marry me and come to New York,' he had said, confronting her with a dilemma she did not know how to handle.

'What about my career?' Caitlin had asked wildly. It was a red herring, but all she could dredge up on the spur of the moment. She was well aware she would be able to continue writing abroad.

'I have no intention of allowing my wife to work,' Matthew had told her grandly. 'Writing trivia about overblown showbusiness personalities is hardly what you would class as a vocation, is it?'

He had not meant to be unkind, she knew that, but his flippant dismissal had made her stop and think. She had never realised that he considered her work so shallow, so unimportant, despite the fact that she was successful and earning a good salary. The guard's shrill whistle disrupted her thoughts. Last-minute passengers scurried along the platform, and there was the slamming of doors further down the carriage. Matthew rose to his feet.

'I'll go now.' His gaze was steady, capturing her eyes. 'Think about us, Cait. I must have a decision on your return. The company needs to know whether I'm going to the States single or married.' He bent to kiss her lightly on the cheek. 'You'd be the ideal wife for a rising young executive. We can go far together.'

As the train pulled slowly out of the station Caitlin waved goodbye, her lower lip caught between her teeth. His retreating figure was so familiar, so loyal, so loving, and yet ... Wearily she picked up the glossy magazine from the table and leafed through the pages. It was a rival publication to the one she wrote for, and as she searched the contents list for the gossip column, the turmoil of her thoughts began to fade. There were four weeks before he required his answer. Four weeks was a long time. Surely she would have come to a decision by then? Her chin lifted decisively—of course she would.

I will have developed leg muscles like knotted ropes by the time I leave here, Caitlin decided wryly as she strode along the lane. It was impossible to calculate how many miles she had walked since arriving two weeks ago, but she was convinced they amounted to hundreds. When she reached a gap in the boundary wall she scrambled through, the high heels of her tan fashion boots skidding on the mossy slabs. For a moment she teetered precariously, clawing at the upright remains of the wall before regaining her balance. If only she had worn her sensible shoes, but they were still sodden from the previous day's excursion.

'Come on, Duke. Look sharp!'

The overweight black Labrador surveyed her from the lane. Chill morning air scythed along her spine like cold steel and she shuddered. Thrusting aside thoughts of the comfortable bed recently deserted, she zipped her anorak closer around her throat and pushed a stray curl beneath the brim of her soft angora hat. A hand was briskly slapped against the thigh of her dark green corduroy trousers. 'Come,' she ordered.

After a moment's hesitation, the old dog swayed amiably through the break in the dry-stone wall to join her.

'Perhaps you do prefer Uncle Desmond's company,' she commented, flexing stiff fingers in white knitted gloves. 'But he's not strong enough yet for morning walks. Give him another week or two, and he'll be rushing you up and down the hills like an express train.'

The dog appeared singularly unimpressed, waiting beside his companion as she shoved her hands deep into her trouser pockets and paused, gazing across the downward slope of the field to the valley beyond and the outline of the Derbyshire hills on the horizon. Despite the biting wind it was May. Spring had budded the trees, and the view was freshly green and brown. Rainwashed limestone walls gleamed palely in the weak sunshine, separating the lush grazing land and ploughed earth into patchwork.

'Enjoy my presence while you can,' Caitlin informed the dog sternly, making her way down the uneven slope. 'I'm returning to London soon.' There was a thoughtful pause. 'And perhaps to Matthew, and then New York. Just be grateful I'm here now and not Joelle. She would never take you out.' Concentration creased her brow as she gingerly crossed the slippery grass.

Together the girl and dog negotiated a second broken wall, and the green slopes were overtaken by woodland which covered the floor of the valley. Duke knew he was free to wander and ambled away, wet black nostrils quivering with excitement at the morning's menu of fresh smells. Caitlin plucked a strand of grass, nibbling at the tender tip. Matthew would have been furious if he had realised Joelle had refused to visit her father, leaving Caitlin little alternative but to follow the dictates of her generous heart.

'I have no intention of disappearing into the darkest depths of the countryside,' Joelle had declared, flicking at her halo of blonde hair with a lacquered nail. 'I shall only visit Daddy if he's on his deathbed, and he's far from it. I'm staying here.' She had glanced around the tiny apartment she and Caitlin shared. 'This is where I belong.'

Morosely Caitlin trudged between the trees, kicking at the turf. Joelle knew exactly where she belonged. In London, trying to carve out a stage career. She sighed. If only her life was so simple to plan, but the future swirled before her like a thick fog. Did she want to marry Matthew and go to New York, or didn't she? If the truth was known, she merely wanted to keep her options open. But why? She knew she loved him, but it seemed a gentle kind of love, too gentle. There had been no clashing of cymbals or impetuous fanfares of desire. Instead their friendship had gradually matured until marriage seemed the inevitable conclusion, at least to Matthew. Irritably Caitlin bit at the grassy sliver with sharp white teeth. At her age she should be more realistic. This yearning for breathless romance was more suited to a teenager. Matthew had proved his devotion over the past two years, what more did she want?

'How the hell do I know?' she bellowed suddenly at the cloud-dappled sky, shaking clenched fists in a frenzy of frustration. What more was there?

At her shout, Duke walked over to investigate and she bent down, scratching him in his favourite spot behind his ears.

'It's all right for you,' she muttered, as he raised soft questioning eyes. Resolutely she straightened and marched on. When they reached the cart-track at the bottom of the valley the dog meandered away to sample

tantalising fragrances on the far side. Caitlin sighed
again, then, as she looked around, her face brightened.
Thick clumps of yellow daffodils were sashaying in the
breeze. It was too good a morning to be introspective.
Kneeling down, she began to pick a handful of the
golden flowers. They'd look so pretty on the cottage
windowsill, and would never be missed. As far as she
knew she was the only person who ever ventured into
the valley, but then she raised her head and listened.

Surely that was the sound of a car engine, coming
near? Someone would have to be crazy to drive along the
valley, for the track was stony and deeply rutted,
littered with pot-holes, presently brimming with muddy
water. In any case it was a dead end, leading only to a
wide meadow where sheep grazed stolidly in verdant
grass. The roar of the approaching engine grew louder.
With a start she remembered Duke, and rose, running
as quickly as she could on her slender heels along the
edge of the track, calling his name.

The throb of the car reached a deafening crescendo,
and as a gleaming electric-blue monster swept round the
bend to her left, the dog appeared ambling slowly along
the centre of the road to her right. Caitlin gave a
terrified yelp, and covered her face with her hands.
There was a thunderous blare of a horn as the steel
monster swept past, drenching her in brown water as its
wheels spun through a puddle. After an ear-splitting
squeal of brakes came a high-pitched whimper and a
series of thuds. The engine cut out. Silence. Fearfully
Caitlin spread her fingers, her heart pounding like a
kettledrum. There was no sign of Duke. The car had
come to rest lopsidedly on a small hillock several yards
ahead. It was a high performance sports model and
looked very expensive. When there was no sign of
movement behind the tinted glass she caught her
breath, and tentatively took a few paces forward.
Perhaps the driver had been injured, or was dead! Her

pulses fluttered alarmingly as she peered through the windscreen, then she took a startled step backwards as the driver's door swung open. Two long muscular legs were thrust out, then a lithe masculine body clad in a track suit. Finally a head of blue-black hair emerged, and two eyes were raised to burn furiously into her like laser beams.

'And what do you think you're playing at?' a clipped voice enquired.

She opened her mouth to snap back an equally angry retort about the stupidity of irresponsible drivers, but the words dried on her lips. That tanned face, with its heavy-lidded eyes, thick black sideburns and arrogant nose was instantly recognisable. At one time in her life Caitlin had felt she knew it better than her own.

'Mr Cameron!' She bit on the Mr, turning it into a term of abuse.

He eyed her narrowly. 'Hell, it's Cait, the infant reporter.' He didn't bother to keep the scorn from his voice.

She drew herself up to her five feet six inches and glared at him.

'You maniac!' she accused. 'You've killed Duke!' Much to her dismay a sob escaped, and she turned away. She had no intention of revealing any weakness to Bryce Cameron. He was the kind of man who traded on others' frailties, as she knew to her cost.

'I don't think so,' he said angrily. 'Though he deserves it, damn dog. He caught a glancing blow from the nearside wing. I imagine he's run off into the bushes to lick his wounds. He'll be back soon.'

The broad chest was rising and falling heavily beneath the zipped jerkin.

'Are you hurt?' Caitlin's question was tentative, asked out of politeness, nothing more. An injured man wouldn't have the energy to be so bad tempered.

'You're to blame if I am,' Bryce snapped out, rising

carefully to his feet to tower above her. With a careful deliberation he moved his hands along each limb in turn, probing the robust muscles as though they were fashioned from spun glass. Periodically he flinched, giving muted gasps of pain. Caitlin's patience began to waver in the face of this flamboyant display of male martyrdom.

'You appear to be in one piece.' His face did seem a little drawn, but she successfully ignored that. 'Not even a flesh wound.' Cynicism frosted her comment. 'I dare say you'll live.'

The black eyes were like flint. 'Big on compassion, aren't you, Sunshine?'

'I'm sure you'll find plenty of others with a far superior bedside manner to mine,' she returned, all milk and honey.

He glared at her. 'Without the seat belt I'd have gone through the windscreen.' He fingered a thin white scar which snaked from the corner of his full lower lip across his jaw. 'And not for the first time.'

'It was your own fault. What on earth do you think you're doing, charging around unmade roads at the speed of light?'

'Practising,' he said, experimentally revolving one massive shoulder.

'Practising!' The reply came out more high-pitched than Caitlin anticipated. She cleared her throat and dropped an octave. 'Do they have road accident events in the Olympics now? No doubt you mow down women and children tomorrow?'

Bryce relaxed against the car, apparently satisfied that he was still intact. 'I'm practising for the next episode of *Slattery*. One of the attractions is the spectacular car chases. They require split-second timing. It's dangerous to leave anything to chance. Safety is paramount in my book.' He made a casual gesture with a large hand. 'We're filming along this valley and using

the old bridge over the river at the end of the meadow.'
A hint of Scots accent burred the edges of his words.
'As I have no desire to flirt with death, I've come here
early to work out the speeds, distances, etc. If you
remember, I do all my own stunts.'

The explanation had been given didactically, and
Caitlin bridled. The *Slattery* series invariably occupied
the number one slot in the television popularity ratings.
It was pure escapism, an exciting piece of make-believe
featuring Bryce Cameron in the title role of the
millionaire detective.

'That's no reason to endanger people's lives,' she
retorted hotly.

'But you, Sunshine, happen to be trespassing. This is
private land and the owner, Sir Quentin Greaves, has
given myself and the film crew *carte blanche* to use it as
and when we wish.' His face glowed with smug
satisfaction. He was well aware he was in the right and
she was in the wrong.

Caitlin wished he had shot through the windscreen
after all.

'You splashed me,' she said, patently ignoring his
words. Her trousers and pale green anorak were
dripping with muddy water. Impetuously she pulled off
the white angora hat, and the glossy curls tumbled
about her face. 'Look, even this is soaking.'

'Don't evade the issue,' Bryce commanded, frowning
down at her. 'You're trespassing *and* stealing.' He
arched a brow at the bedraggled bunch of daffodils in
her fist.

'Nobody will miss them. Nobody comes here,' she
retaliated.

'*I* come here.'

'Well, have the rotten things.' Crossly she pushed the
flowers at him.

'And be charged with aiding and abetting? No, thank
you.'

His eyes gleamed with amusement at her uncontrolled anger. He looked so complacent, so sure of himself, that Caitlin felt like hitting him. The fancy car, the velour black track suit were typical Bryce, she thought contemptuously. She had to admit that he had style. As dream hero of thousands of women, he instinctively knew what was right for his image. Charisma was a word often attributed by journalists searching for a clue to his lethal appeal, and it was apt.

Slowly he surveyed her, then uncoiled and stretched out his arms above his head, smiling lazily. It was a deliberate gesture to make her aware of him sexually, and as he flexed the long muscled torso Caitlin stared back blankly. He could try that trick on other women. She was not impressed. Bryce grinned at the determined lack of reaction. In the furry black suit he resembled a sleek and luxuriant panther, so that Caitlin would not have been surprised if his eyes had flashed yellow, and he had stretched out an unsheathed paw to rip her anorak to shreds. But that wasn't his style, she remembered. His claws were always sheathed. He preferred to torment his victims rather than attack outright. She tightened her mouth into a disapproving line. He had treated her like a kitten in the past, tossing her around to suit his pleasure, making her purr because she hadn't the sense to spit. Well, that kitten had grown up.

Bryce smoothed a reverent hand over the glistening bonnet of the sports car. 'I presume you can afford to pay if there's any damage? Repairs will cost a bomb. It's a Maserati, a pedigree car.'

'Duke's a pedigree dog,' Caitlin retaliated.

'But hardly worth over twenty thousand pounds?'

'You can't measure animals, or people, in money,' she said primly.

'Come now,' he drawled. 'What about footballers, or

even Slattery? He's a very valuable property, he's created millions.'

Her eyes glittered with disdain. 'Tell me, Mr Cameron, don't you find it impossible at times to differentiate between the charming Slattery and yourself?' Her words dripped venom.

He pursed his mouth, considering her question, then threw back his dark head and laughed, his teeth white and strong against his tan. 'Coming from you, Caitlin Saunders, that's a very strange thing to ask.' He lowered his voice, the smile coming through. 'I well remember a naïve young lady who wasn't aware of the difference two years ago.'

Caitlin was furious to feel herself crimsoning. The expression in his eyes showed no mercy.

'Are you still so delightfully innocent?' he asked, the corner of his lips lifting with amusement.

'No!' She shot back the reply without thinking.

'So you're a woman of experience?' he chuckled.

Caitlin frowned. There was no way she would admit any shortcomings to Bryce, and in his eyes being innocent was a definite minus.

'I've been around.' It was a plastic reply.

'You can handle whatever's thrown at you now?' His question sounded like a challenge.

'I can,' she assured him haughtily, ignoring the laughter which continued to tug at the side of his mouth.

He reached out a hand and touched her hair, disregarding the way she tensed.

'You've changed. I like the curls. The schoolmarm look you had before didn't turn me on at all.' His expert eyes swept her snugly-clad body. 'Put you in a bikini, and you'd be a real Slattery girl.'

'No, thanks,' she said frostily. 'There's more to life than being an accessory.'

A Slattery girl was featured in every episode of the series. Usually a tall blonde, with a full figure and windswept brain. They poured themselves into his cars, his swimming pools, his beds and were breathlessly seduced in the sixty minutes available. Caitlin suspected they were equally breathlessly seduced by Bryce after the cameras stopped rolling. Probably that took only sixty minutes, too. Joelle had been trying to land a part as a Slattery girl for months.

With a shrug Bryce turned to the car. 'I'll check that this expensive accessory is roadworthy, and then we'll search for that hound of yours.'

He walked slowly around the Maserati, squatting down on his haunches to inspect tyres, lights and undercarriage in great detail with an experienced eye. Eventually he straightened up. 'All clear.'

'Does it belong to you?' Caitlin asked as she walked beside him along the track.

He shook his head. 'It's hired for the series. I'm using it until we finish filming. Frank Stern, the director, wants me to push the Slattery image all the way; he reckons it's good publicity.' He glanced back over his shoulder. 'The insurance is phenomenal.'

Caitlin peered through the trees and shouted. For several minutes they searched, each calling loudly, until there was a rustle of leaves and Duke emerged from the bushes, limping slightly, his tail between his legs, a subdued expression in his brown eyes. Caitlin knelt down and held him close, crooning words of comfort, while Bryce ran his fingers over the wavering paw.

'Seems okay. No bones broken.'

'Then why is he limping?' she demanded as they returned to the track, Duke hobbling beside them on three legs.

'I've no idea.'

'Slattery knew when *his* dog's leg was fractured. He put it into a splint,' she announced triumphantly, remembering a past episode.

'Slattery is a fictitious character,' Bryce reminded her

in scathing tones. 'In any case that was a Dobermann, and obviously its leg wasn't really broken.'

'But can't you even remember how to fix a splint?' she implored.

A large hand encircled her arm, dragging her to a halt.

'Duke's leg is fine. He doesn't need running repairs,' he said flatly.

Caitlin pulled herself away. The hard grip of his fingers was disturbing. 'I'm worried about him,' she justified.

'You're more concerned about the damn dog than you are about me.' The accusation was flung at her.

'You can look after yourself,' she said coldly. 'He's a dumb animal.'

'That makes two of you.' He raised a sardonic brow. 'I'll drive you both to the vet's.'

His suggestion made sense, and Caitlin was forced to agree, asking only if they might call at her uncle's home first to explain her absence. Bryce reversed the Maserati on to the track, stopping beside the girl and the dog.

'Get in,' he said tersely, his tanned face grim as he leaned across and pushed open the passenger door.

She cast him a sidelong glance. 'What's the matter?'

'A fat old dog like that has no place inside a beautiful car like this,' he grumbled. 'For heaven's sake watch he doesn't chew or scratch anything, or shed hairs all over the place.'

'You wouldn't complain if it was a blonde,' Caitlin tossed in sweetly.

'I would if she moulted.'

At the speed Bryce drove it took less than ten minutes to cover the circuitous route back down the valley, through the village and along the two-mile stretch to her uncle's cottage. As he manhandled the wheel he plied questions. Caitlin edited the answers for she had no intention of revealing too much of herself to him. She'd learnt a few tricks since the last time they clashed.

'You're still with the same magazine?' he said. It was more a statement than a question.

'Yes.'

'But no longer the infant reporter?'

'I'm second in line to Alison Frobisher now.'

Bryce raised his dark brows. 'Very impressive.' He winced as the dog slithered around uncaringly on Caitlin's knees. 'I've read some of your stuff. It's quite good.'

'Thank you, kind sir.' Caitlin bobbed her head sarcastically, making the curls dance at the nape of her neck.

He threw her a disapproving frown at the mockery. 'You've come a long way since you interviewed me.'

'If everything had depended on that meeting, Mr Cameron, I would have gone a long way into oblivion.'

'You were an amateur in those days, but now you're a professional.' He studied her from beneath thick black lashes. 'You appear to be a formidable force.'

She couldn't decide whether he was laughing at her again, but gave him the benefit of the doubt.

'I am,' she assured him as the car came to a halt outside the wicket gate. 'Now if you would be kind enough to lift the dog off my knee, I'll go inside and tell my uncle what's happened.'

Climbing from the driving seat Bryce came round to open her door. He stooped to pick up the Labrador, but before he could grasp him Duke jumped nimbly out and trotted off up the path on four sturdy legs. He gave a laugh of disbelief.

'There's an actor for you!' he said, watching as the rotund backside swaggered towards the front door.

'And he's male,' Caitlin added pointedly, stepping on to the pavement.

Bryce swung himself back into the driving seat. 'No

need to visit the vet's now. I'll return to my practising.'

'Shall I pressgang a bevy of little old ladies for you to knock down?'

'Don't push me too hard, Sunshine.' His black eyes roamed her face for a moment before he slipped the key into the ignition and roared away.

Caitlin stared after him. He hadn't changed at all. Bryce was still arrogantly confident, it was she who was different. Two years ago she'd been unsophisticated and unsure of herself, but now . . . She gave a little chuckle. Now she was well able to deal with Bryce and others like him.

Her uncle was busily preparing breakfast when she entered the kitchen.

'Why didn't you stay in bed while you had the chance?' she rebuked, removing her anorak and taking the cups from their shelf on the Welsh dresser.

'Don't fuss,' he smiled. 'It's high time I learnt to be independent again. Besides, I had to get up to answer the phone.'

Caitlin glanced at him questioningly.

'It was Maurice,' he told her. 'He wanted to know if you would call in at the *Bugle* today. He wondered if you would do a couple of articles for him.'

The *Bugle* was the local newspaper. It enjoyed a regular readership, scattered over the county. Maurice Gill, the editor, was an old friend of Desmond's, and when he had heard Caitlin would be staying in the area for a while he had dropped hefty hints that any freelance articles from her would be gratefully received. Once she had satisfied herself that her uncle didn't need twenty-four-hour attendance, she had offered her services, and quickly found herself knee-deep in requests to cover everything from Scout jumble sales to the local dispute over the siting of a new reservoir. It had been refreshing to return to grass roots for at times the material she wrote for the gossip columns of the magazine disturbed her. She had grown weary of oversize egos and miniature talent, though she would never admit it, especially to Matthew. There was a tendency for showbusiness personalities to take themselves far too seriously. They would ramble on for hours on end about the meaningful role their talent played in life, and often she found herself writing, tongue firmly in cheek. What a relief it was to speak to ordinary people, like herself, who weren't obsessed with their looks, their clothes, their lovelife.

Uncle Desmond reached for the coffee pot. His movements were firm now, and Caitlin was delighted to see a touch of colour in his paper-pale features.

'Who brought you home? I heard the noise of an engine,' he said. 'It sounded as though it packed a hefty horsepower.'

'Bryce Cameron, the actor. A *Slattery* episode is being filmed here, and he's working on one of the fast-car sequences.'

'I've heard about him. Elsie, I mean Mrs Richards,' he cleared his throat selfconsciously, 'tells me he's staying at the King's Head. He's the talk of the village, and his presence has livened everyone up no end.' He grinned. 'I've been subjected to a daily report on his activities. Elsie would love to meet him—I think she has a soft spot for him.'

Caitlin allowed herself a small smile. So Bryce had yet another admirer. They certainly came in all ages and sizes, and now a plump grey-haired lady in her sixties had been added to the list. No doubt the King's Head, the local hotel, was reverberating to the dull thud of women falling to the floor as Bryce strolled by.

'Is he alone?' she asked, slicing into buttered toast, 'or is some exotic girl-friend in attendance?'

'Alone at present, but I believe the rest of the

television people arrive this afternoon. Eleanor Halbert will be coming.'

Caitlin raised her shapely brows. The actress had been linked, off and on, with Bryce for years. What capacity would Eleanor be filling in Derbyshire—co-star or lover, or both? She had certainly proved to have more staying-power than Bryce's other women, but then, Caitlin admitted, she was a cut above the rest. Although cast in the common mould—blonde and beautiful—she was keenly intelligent and, surprisingly, four years older than the actor. Usually he preferred younger women who were putty in his expert hands. Eleanor Halbert was far too strong a character to fall into that category.

'Is Mr Cameron a friend of yours?' Desmond asked hopefully.

'Definitely not. I interviewed him once, ages ago when I was very green, and it was a complete disaster. Occasionally I see him around in London, but I always keep my distance.'

'You don't care for him?' He read her tone accurately.

'He's exactly like Slattery, the character he portrays— charmingly amoral. He doesn't give a damn about people's feelings.'

'Elsie would still like to meet him,' her uncle persisted. 'Couldn't you persuade him to call round? It would make her very happy.'

'No,' Caitlin replied testily, then her voice softened. 'You seem very eager to please Mrs Richards,' she teased. 'Do you fancy her?'

Desmond flushed. 'She's a widow, all alone like me. She's been very kind, especially since my stroke.'

Caitlin smiled. It would be a weight off her mind if Uncle Desmond married again. Her own parents lived too far away to visit more than a couple of times a year, and she always felt uneasy at the thought of his living alone, despite Joelle's airy assurances that he was perfectly contented with his dog and his garden.

After breakfast she changed from the mud-stained cords into a topaz-coloured sweat shirt and culottes, then put her notebook and pencil into her leather shoulderbag.

'Why not take the car?' Desmond suggested, as she ran downstairs.

'No, thank you.' She slipped her arms into her brown suede jacket. 'The magic touch with that old wreck still eludes me. I'd probably end up being towed home in disgrace, like last time.'

'It can be temperamental,' her uncle admitted with a smile. His dilapidated Ford was of an uncertain age and behaviour. It displayed the whims of an elderly prima donna, and no amount of coaxing from Caitlin could persuade it to start when it was not in the mood.

'Perhaps I should sling it on the scrap-heap,' he mused. 'But it would be like parting from an old friend.'

'Old enemy!' Caitlin retorted. 'I'll walk down to the village. The exercise will do me good.' More knotted-rope muscles, she thought with a grimace.

The spring sunshine had warmed the air, and Caitlin released the buttons on her jacket as she walked along. Newly minted leaves were bursting on the trees, and fluffy white lambs gambolled beside their mothers. She stopped and peered over the hedge for a few minutes to watch a trio of leggy colts. It was so easy to forget nature's yearly recital when you lived in a city, she realised with a sigh of regret. As she walked on she thrust a hand into her pocket, and her fingers brushed against the morning's letter from Matthew. She took it out and slid an index finger beneath the flap. There was really no need to read it. She already knew what it would say—that he loved her, and missed her, and would she hurry up and decide to marry him. Caitlin scanned the neat writing. Matthew was predictable to the extreme, as methodical in his personal life as he was with his columns of figures. Her relationship with him was so ordered, it was almost a habit. She sighed. But it was difficult to imagine life without him. Even when she had been tempted away into a temporary alliance with a more dashing partner, he had accepted her back without recrimination, picking up their regular dates as though she'd never strayed. And she always returned, that was the point. Other young men may have offered more excitement, but they had never offered such patient love and security. Caitlin thrust the letter impatiently back into its envelope. There were still two more weeks, plenty of time to reach a decision.

The village streets were busy. It was both market and pension day, and there was an influx of elderly farmers and their wives from outlying areas, as well as strangers from the industrial Midlands who had motored in to buy fresh vegetables and meat for their freezers. As she passed the King's Head, her eyes whisked over the cars parked in the forecourt. No sign of the electric-blue Maserati. Idly she wondered what Bryce thought of Derbyshire. Presumably, like Joelle, he considered it deadly dull. Life here was a far cry from the slick night life and elegant society whirl of London. Caitlin frowned. If her memory was correct, he owned a chain of garages in Scotland. It appeared a down-to-earth investment, but doubtless he left all business decisions to some well-paid manager. It was unlikely that he would bother his handsome head with problems of staffing and cash flow. He was a wealthy playboy, exactly like Slattery, she decided with a derisive curl of her lip.

She turned into a narrow alleyway between two gritstone buildings and made her way up the rickety wooden steps at the end which led to the *Bugle*'s offices.

'How's it going, Cait?' Paul Land, a junior reporter

in his late teens, smiled a greeting as she entered the general office.

'Fine.' She perched on the corner of his desk, swinging a slender ankle. 'How are you progressing with the court reports?'

He grimaced at the sheaf of papers on his desk, and Caitlin laughed.

'It's good training, even if it is deadly boring,' she told him. 'You have to make sure your facts are accurate, otherwise there'd soon be some irate guy yelling for blood because you'd attributed him with careless driving when he'd only parked on double yellow lines.'

'I suppose so.' Paul rocked back on two legs of his chair. 'How long did you do this kind of stuff?'

'Two or three years, then I struck lucky. I won a competition, and was offered a magazine job in London.'

'London,' he echoed dreamily. 'If only I could get there!'

'The streets aren't paved entirely with gold,' she teased. 'I did months and months of humdrum, fact-finding work at the start. Even now it's not all celebrity interviews.'

'I wish there was a nice juicy murder in the village. Perhaps Mr Gill would give me a shot at it, and I'd become famous overnight. Paul Land, ace crime reporter,' he said wistfully.

'Slattery's here. You could interview him.'

Paul pushed a blond forelock from his brow and grinned. 'Have you seen his car! Isn't it fantastic! I'd sell my soul for a drive in that. If only I could wangle an introduction to him.'

Caitlin silenced a stab of irritation. She had no intention of revealing her tenuous connection with Bryce. It was bad enough that Uncle Desmond had already pushed Mrs Richards' case. If people realised she was on talking terms with him, she'd have the butcher, the baker and the local Tupperware lady angling for a contact.

'Is Mr Gill out?' she asked, glancing towards the opaque glass-walled cubicle at the end of the room. 'My uncle said he has a couple of assignments for me.'

'He'll be back in a few minutes. He's across at the market. There's a dispute among the stall holders, so he's listening to everyone's point of view.'

Caitlin tugged at the waistband of her culottes. 'Have you any idea what he wants me to write about?'

Paul nodded. 'It's Sir Quentin's charity fête on Saturday, up at Greaves Court. Mr Gill wondered if you would lend a hand.' He pulled a wry face. 'It's all high-pressure stuff. Reporting the winner of the fruit cake competition, who grows the best chrysanths, naming the most bouncing baby—ugh!'

'It'll be good fun,' she said encouragingly.

'Unless it rains.' He looked gloomy. 'You should have been here last year. It poured down. One of the marquees collapsed, and a dozen cars were stuck in the mud.'

Caitlin giggled. There was the sound of heavy footsteps on the wooden staircase, and a bulky, middle-aged man burst into the room.

'Those stall holders are going at it hell for leather,' he announced, wiping his red face with a large handkerchief. 'Talk about tempers running high! You'd wonder how anyone could become so irate over a few sticks of wood and a canvas cover.' He turned to Paul. 'How about making us a cup of tea, lad?'

'Yes, Mr Gill.' Paul disappeared towards the kitchen.

'Thanks for coming in, Cait,' Maurice smiled, putting his arm around her shoulders and guiding her into his cubicle. He sat down behind a desk littered with an array of reference books, files and letters, and indicated a chair.

'We shall miss you when you go back to London,

lass. You've been a life-saver. Paul is a good kid, but he needs more experience before I can really let him loose.'

'I understand you want me to help him write up the charity fête at Greaves Court?'

'If you would. It'll be a nice day out if the weather behaves itself. There's dancing around the Maypole, sideshows, something for all the family. It should attract more crowds than usual this year, as I understand Sir Quentin's prevailed on that Bryce Cameron to open it.'

Caitlin's hazel eyes widened. Mundane village events seemed incompatible with Bryce's high-powered lifestyle, but then she remembered that the television episode was being filmed on Sir Quentin's land. It must be a case of 'you scratch my back, and I'll scratch yours'.

'Have you seen the car that lad drives?' Maurice Gill demanded, making her clench her teeth in exasperation. 'It's a beauty. It certainly attracts attention, so does he for that matter. The King's Head hasn't done so much trade for years. The bar's heaving with women trying to catch a glimpse of him.'

'Whatever turns you on.' She wrinkled her nose dismissively.

'You mean he doesn't appeal to you?' Maurice looked astonished.

'Not in the slightest. If I was marooned on a desert island with him, I'd go and drown myself.'

The editor cleared his throat. 'Well, actually that brings me to a second job I'd like you to do.' He glanced at her warily. 'I wondered if you'd interview Bryce Cameron for me? I've had a word with him, and he's perfectly happy to spare an hour or so.'

CHAPTER TWO

A GLEAMING chestnut curl was flipped from her shoulder. 'Why not send Paul?' she suggested lightly. 'It would be good experience for him.'

'The boy wouldn't know how to handle a man like Cameron. He's too star-struck. He'd probably stutter, or dry up completely.' Maurice laced his hands on the top of his head and smiled persuasively. 'You've interviewed masses of entertainment folk, it's your stock in trade. You can deal with a high-flyer like Cameron.' He winked. 'You know the kind of mumbo-jumbo to ask, about his love life and all. That's what folk are interested in. He's supposed to be quite a lad with the ladies. The *Bugle* could do with a boost in circulation, and I reckon Bryce Cameron's sexual antics would do the trick.'

Caitlin's fingernails bit sharply into her palms; another illusion had gone up in smoke! So village folk were just as interested in the salacious aspects of life as everyone else!

'I've asked Bob to take some photographs,' Maurice continued. 'He's going round this afternoon. We'll have a blow-up of Cameron and the Maserati on the front page, and some kind of photospread on the centre pages.'

'How many words do you want?'

'Around two thousand. I've not decided yet if we'll use it all in one issue. Perhaps we could string it out into a series, keep it on the boil for a few weeks.' He rubbed his hands together gleefully. 'You watch, sales will soar. I'll tell the boys to print extra copies.'

Caitlin raised a scathing brow. Alleluia for Bryce! It

was a wonder Maurice didn't rush round to the hotel and kiss his feet.

'When do I interview him?' Her no-nonsense tone jolted into his happy surmising.

'Around ten tomorrow morning at the King's Head.'

The sun had disappeared behind the clouds and it had begun to fleck with rain when she emerged from the newspaper offices. Caitlin pulled up her collar, mumbling under her breath about the waywardness of the English climate. The walk back to the cottage seemed endless, and although the rain was light she almost wished she had risked bringing out the old Ford. A black mood, like a sense of doom, crept over her. The prospect of interviewing Bryce Cameron was unsettling. He displayed an uncanny knack of bringing out the worst in her, and their meeting was destined to be a battle of wills. Professionally, she was well aware that it was not the best basis for an interview. The key to good copy was a relaxed atmosphere, but how could she ever relax in Bryce's company?

Her thoughts flashed back to the first time they had met. Then Bryce had emerged the outright winner, but she was determined that he wouldn't get the better of her again. There was no reason at all why she shouldn't have her revenge. The side of her mouth lifted in delight at the idea, and her pace quickened. She would write an exposé. It would be easy to strip aside the superficial gloss and reveal Bryce and the Slattery image for the candyfloss they really were. The tone of her article would be tongue in cheek, jokey even, but with sufficient bite to indicate that Bryce and the character he played so expertly were merely identical properties, packaged to suit the public, but not worthy of serious consideration. Caitlin chuckled. Why not! Why shouldn't she make fun of the dream hero, she thought defensively. It might not be strictly ethical, but she felt entitled to batter his career a little—after all, he'd almost ruined hers.

A plan began to form in her head. She'd use his own weapons, and with the professionalism she now controlled, would ruthlessly present a side of Bryce which his fans had never suspected. Revenge would be sweet!

Born and bred in a small country town, Caitlin was, she knew, what was termed a 'late developer'. As the only daughter of doting parents she had been lovingly protected throughout her childhood, and even when she had shown the flair and determination to become a journalist, her job had been on a local newspaper, working within the secure confines of an area she had always known. Her career, like her life, promised to be respectable, structured and somewhat limited.

Winning first prize in a national competition organised by a leading women's magazine changed all that. Abruptly she was uprooted from a predictable world to one which astonished, thrilled and threw her completely off balance. Living in London reminded her of being caught up in a revolving door, never knowing whether you were destined to be hurled out into comfortable warmth or biting chill.

'Thank goodness you can share a flat with Joelle,' Caitlin's mother had said, with a sigh of relief. 'At least you'll know somebody. She'll look after you and show you the ropes.'

Mrs Saunders' hair would have turned stark white overnight if she had realised the kind of ropes Joelle coiled. Although only a year older than Caitlin's twenty-two, she was light years ahead in matters of experience. Caitlin wasn't daunted. Quickly she adapted to late-night parties, racy gossip, the hordes of sultry young men who rushed in and out of her cousin's bedroom like ticket collectors. As Joelle taught her the

tricks of good grooming and latest fashion trends, so
her appearance gained a patina of sophistication.
Inwardly, however, her principles remained unchanged.
The sultry bedfellows were not for her.

It had been a relief when she met Matthew. He was
her kind of person. He didn't slide a practised hand
along her thigh, or breathe whisky fumes. Matthew was
respectable, and at first she clung to him like a
drowning sailor to a lifebelt. With Matthew she felt
safe. But perversely, as time passed, Caitlin began to
wish he would at least show a desire to slide his hand
along her leg, or suggest something more outrageous
than a regular dinner or film date. No such luck.
Instead he edged the conversation around to the merits
of Georgian-style detached houses, and mortgages, and
his promising career prospects.

The journalistic side of her new life was something of
a shock, too. Although she possessed a talent for
writing and was well versed in factual reporting, she
had never dealt in personalities. Now she was thrust
into a world where lifestyles and love affairs were of
prime importance, for she was assigned to the
showbusiness section of the magazine. Alison Frobisher,
a large flamboyant lady with a vocabulary like a
navvy's, was the chief columnist.

'Listen, learn and keep your mouth shut, Honeybun,'
she instructed as together they hurtled around the city
reporting on film stars and ballet dancers and one-hit
pop singers. Alison appreciated enthusiasm, and
quickly took Caitlin into her confidence, discussing
ways of wringing interest from a seemingly dull topic,
or probing veins of rich material.

'You have to be a bit of everything in this line,' the
older woman declared, searching unplumbed depths of
her handbag for a Biro. 'Detective, court jester, best
friend, Mother Superior.'

Reporting came easy to Alison, she'd been on Fleet

Street for years. She had a reputation. It wasn't so simple for a newcomer.

The Bryce Cameron interview had been arranged between his agent and the magazine. *Slattery* had recently grabbed top rating, and a second run was scheduled for the autumn. Bryce had become famous. He was in great demand. A cover photograph of him, and a provocative article, would combine to publicise the television series, and sell more magazines. Everyone would be happy.

Alison scribbled a list of questions with Caitlin at her shoulder.

'Bryce is a nice guy. He appreciates that reporters have a living to earn, and he always co-operates. The first time I questioned him was ages ago when he was doing Ibsen.'

Caitlin's gaping mouth made her laugh.

'He has done serious work. Bryce was a respectable actor before *Slattery*. He started out in repertory, then carried spears. He's worked hard, he deserves this ten-year overnight success.' Her final notes were jotted down. 'There,' she said with a satisfied grin. 'First thing tomorrow we'll shoot off and see what's new with the gorgeous Mr Cameron.'

But the following morning Alison croaked down the telephone that she had caught bronchitis, and Caitlin was to do the interview alone.

'I'm not ready,' she pleaded, panic-stricken.

'Yes, you are.' The columnist sounded like a weary bullfrog. 'You've been to dozens of interviews with me. The list of questions is on my desk, so just ask them. It's straightforward. He won't eat you alive.'

Caitlin wasn't so sure.

Bryce Cameron lived in a third-floor apartment in a discreetly luxurious building off Park Lane. Her stubby heels sank inches into the plush carpet as she entered the high-ceilinged vestibule, and her heart quaked when a lordly commissionaire, in morning suit and top hat, approached to enquire if he could assist. With a shaky smile she gave the number of Bryce's apartment. The man eyed her curiously and she realised she was not the usual type of woman to visit the actor at home.

'I've come to do an interview,' she explained weakly. The commissionaire sniffed contemptuously, and the superficial confidence, so recently acquired, dissolved beneath his scrutiny. Caitlin rushed forward into the lift with quivering limbs. What on earth was she doing here? With a nervous tongue she moistened her lips and studied the reflection in the mirror as the lift slowly ascended. Her hair was combed back into a neat bun at the back of her head, all wispy curls carefully tucked in. She had hurriedly applied extra lipstick and mascara in a vain attempt at maturity. With clammy fingers she tugged at the white lace collar of her navy suit. If only she'd had more time to prepare. Her fragile poise needed the boost of a fashionable hairstyle and one of her more sophisticated outfits. As it was she looked disgustingly juvenile and innocent, and that certainly wasn't the image she wished to project.

When he opened the door it was instantly apparent Bryce Cameron was not impressed either.

'Where's Alison?' he demanded, turning his back and walking away into his apartment, leaving Caitlin on the threshold wondering what to do. She closed the front door and followed him.

'Mrs Frobisher has bronchitis. She sent me.'

His size surprised her. He was much taller than he appeared on the television screen, and broader, too. Suspicious black eyes made an inspection.

'Seems that reporters, like policemen, get younger every day. I presume you have left school.'

'Yes, I have,' Caitlin protested, feeling her cheeks burn. 'I'm quite experienced.'

'I bet you are.'

She didn't know how to answer that.

Bryce halted before her in the hallway. He planted his feet firmly apart and folded his arms, then gave her a long, level look. He was wearing beige slacks and a silky turtle-neck sweater in dark brown. There was a hostile pause as he considered the options.

Caitlin chewed at her lip as she waited.

'Mrs Frobisher might recover by the end of the week,' she suggested hopefully. 'The deadline's not too desperate.'

'Perhaps you have time to fool around, Sunshine,' he informed her curtly, 'but I don't. This afternoon I'm flying up to Scotland for a fortnight. After that I'm filming.' He made an impatient movement with a large hand. 'Oh, what the hell, let's get on with it.'

A strong smell of paint filled Caitlin's nostrils as he led her into a vast, creamy-carpeted lounge. Most of the furniture had been removed, there were no curtains at the windows and the newly papered walls were bare.

'Sorry about this,' he mumbled, though his diffident expression belied the apology. 'I've only recently moved here. The decorators are in.'

Two pale lemon armchairs faced each other, isolated on the desert of shaggy carpet. Caitlin took the one he indicated and pulled out her list of questions. Bryce settled back in his chair, crossing long legs and drumming impatient fingers on the velvet pile.

She cleared her throat. 'Well, Mr Slattery——' she began.

With one predatory surge Bryce leapt forward to engulf her, taut hands grasping the arms of her chair, forming a prison.

'*Slattery!*' he snarled, his mouth twisting with anger. His face was only menacing inches from hers, and she could feel the fieriness of his breath on her skin. He seemed to be consumed by an irrational rage, and Caitlin cowered back in terror. The mistake had been easily made. She had seen him frequently on television where he *was* the millionaire detective.

'Get this straight,' he ground out. 'Slattery is a figment of the imagination. The only place he exists is on celluloid. My name is Cameron, Bryce Cameron, and don't you dare forget it for one moment!' He looked as though he was about to pounce and tear her apart. 'I'm sick to death of Slattery,' he said thinly. 'I'm *me!*'

Her already zinging nerves screamed as she gulped an incoherent apology. She was expecting more angry words when, without warning, he suddenly released his hold on her chair and straightened. For a few tense moments he prowled before her, then he halted and rubbed the edge of his jaw with a thoughtful hand. The fury melted like snow in the sun, and his dark eyes gleamed.

'But why not?' he murmured, almost to himself. 'If you want Slattery, you can damn well have Slattery.' His features spread into a smile, and Caitlin found herself gratefully responding. The tension in the air lessened palpably. He was a good-looking man, and the charisma he displayed on the screen was even more powerful in real life.

'You're a very pretty girl,' he announced, his eyes lazily trickling over her, removing the trim navy suit and every other wisp of clothing. 'When you are older . . .' His deep voice trailed away, making her flush. She hadn't come here to be inspected. Alison had said he was a complex character, and so he was. Caitlin didn't know what to make of him. Seduction was doubtless a biological necessity to a man like Bryce, but she was well aware innocent young women were not his type. The cuttings she had quickly scanned before leaving the office had revealed a procession of glamorous blondes, all women experienced in the ways of the world. The wandering eyes continued to dissect her, and she turned away, looking anywhere but at him.

'I shan't bite.' The comment was full of silent laughter. 'I presume you are above the age of consent?'

Caitlin's astonishment showed in her face. He was playing some game and she hadn't read the rules.

'I'm nearly twenty-three,' she declared, furiously adding a good nine months.

With one swift movement he made a grab for her hand and pulled her upright beside him. 'So old!' Two mocking brows were raised as he placed his hands on her waist.

'Shall we start the interview?' she asked hurriedly. She had no idea what would happen next, and whatever it was she wasn't sure if she would like it. Alison should have warned her that he was dangerous.

'Relax a little, you're too uptight,' he crooned, sliding strong hands slowly down her back, pulling her close. Caitlin froze. The hardness of his male length against her prompted an instinctive feminine response. For a moment she was tempted to yield to his masculinity and lean against the firmly-muscled body. She glanced up in bewilderment. Damn him! He knew all the time what he was doing, she could see it in his smiling, taunting eyes. Raising determined hands she pushed him away. He abandoned her happily, without resistance.

'Shall we start the interview?' she said again, sitting down and trying to control the trembling which threatened to reveal her distress. Flames seemed to be leaping from her skin. Bryce was despicable. As an actor he was totally aware of his sexuality, controlling and using it whenever it suited him. She recognised that it contributed in a large part to *Slattery*'s success. His sex appeal, when paraded against a backdrop of exotic locations, elegant women, expensive gadgets, was a potent force. And now he was using it on her! Irritation made her lift her head and glare at him. He grinned back with unholy glee. He seemed to regard her presence as a joke, deriving malicious delight from her confusion. With a steadying intake of breath she wished she was confident and experienced like Joelle. Her cousin would have brushed the incident aside with some casual banter. Joelle wouldn't be hot-faced and shaking. As she picked up her notebook Bryce glanced at the heavy gold watch on his wrist.

'I'm due out in forty-five minutes. I'll have to change. Can you hang on?'

Without waiting for a reply he disappeared through a door which presumably led to his bedroom. Caitlin groaned inwardly. The interview wasn't straightforward at all. How did you cope with a man who swung from anger to teasing with only a second's lapse between? He had no right to treat her so disgracefully. Her pulses raced as she remembered the confident authority of his hands, pulling her against him. She had never met a man who exhibited such sexual virility, and was furious with herself for reacting. She was well aware it had been merely a whim which had prompted him to hold her, and yet her traitorous body had leapt at his touch. She chewed a fingernail reflectively. The sooner she was out of his apartment the better.

There was a sound of running water, then the tap was turned off and Bryce returned, clad only in blue denims, a towel casually draped across his broad shoulders. The golden skin glistened, and he dabbed at it as he sauntered across the acres of carpet and sat down. Nonchalantly he swung a muscular leg over one arm of the chair. The jeans must have been glued on, for they outlined his thighs in a manner which left his masculinity in no doubt. Caitlin was mesmerised. It was becoming difficult to breathe. Then she realised that his eyes were on her. He was coolly assessing her reaction, a taunting curl at the corner of his mouth. She flushed and looked away.

'Are you wondering how I get to look like this, Sunshine?' he asked offhandedly, the dark eyes brimming with some private joke. The parched, constricting muscles in her throat made speech impossible. She bent her head to examine her patent shoes, and wished she was ten thousand miles away.

'I'll tell you,' he drawled. 'To keep in good physical condition I swim five miles a day, jog for twenty, and work out in a gym three times a week. I'm also a karate fanatic.' He raked jet-black hair from his brow. 'Write it all down, there's a good girl. That's what you're here for.'

Feeling utterly foolish she grabbed her pencil and began to scribble his words. Then she remembered the small tape recorder in her bag, it would be wise to employ that, too. Hurriedly she placed it on her lap and pressed the switch. When Bryce laughed she raised her head.

'We're yards apart,' he pointed out. 'You'll never pick anything up from that distance.' He ran brown fingers provocatively along his denim-clad leg from thigh to knee. 'You could always come and sit here.'

Caitlin felt dizzy, but her 'No, thank you,' was firm.

'Wait a minute,' he instructed, and strode from the room, only to return seconds later with a low, smoked-glass coffee table which he placed by his chair. 'Put the machine on here.'

She complied, scuttling back to her seat as quickly as a frightened rabbit. The firm naked chest with its smooth muscles and curly dark hair seemed to be imprinting itself on her memory cells. She wished he'd wear a shirt.

'Fire away,' he said, with the ghost of a chuckle.

Caitlin fired away, though the questions resembled damp squibs rather than bullets. Alison had a knack of turning interviews into friendly chats, where conversation flowed spontaneously, but despite Bryce's prompt replies Caitlin knew her questioning was stilted.

Her finger moved to the next query. 'When are you

planning to settle down, Mr Cameron?' she asked primly.

'You mean when am I going to start behaving myself?' he teased. 'When am I going to tell all those luscious blondes to stop climbing into my bed?'

Confusion and embarrassment tightened her chest. Bryce eyed the carefully bowed head with amusement.

'I don't intend to settle down—ever. Why should I restrict myself to one woman when there's a world outside full of them?'

The reply was jotted down. Blindly she progressed to the next question. 'Do you believe your birth sign rules your actions?' She shook her head in despair. 'This is impossible. Reading out from a list doesn't work.'

'Don't worry, you're doing fine.' He gave a smile of encouragement. 'So what if some of the queries are banal? I'm used to it.'

His good nature was surprising. Many other celebrities would have shown her the door long ago for her unprofessional conduct, and rightly so, but Bryce calmly accepted her gauche questioning and trotted out answers as though reading from a book. The only time he showed any reluctance was when she deserted the subject of *Slattery* and asked about his previous acting career. Then he shied away, giving brief factual replies. It was obvious he much preferred to talk about the present character he was playing and that, she decided, was really what the interview was about. As he produced wisecracks and quotable quotes with an amiable grin, Caitlin began to cool down and regain a measure of poise. She was grateful for his co-operation. Now that he had abandoned the role of tormentor-in-chief he was friendly and approachable, and she warmed towards him. He sprawled in the chair like a superb jungle cat, his hair glossily blue-black, his powerful physique pulsating with health. The gruelling exercise regime certainly kept him in fine shape.

'That's all, thank you,' Caitlin said at last.

'You're positive? Do you want me to repeat anything? Be certain you have all you need.'

She was touched by his consideration and smiled.

'If you require further information or want to change anything, contact my agent. Here's the number.' He scribbled it down.

'You're very kind.' Caitlin stuffed the recorder and notebook away. After the fraught beginning Bryce had made the interview easy. She had grasped enough know-how to realise that some of his quotes were gems. It's a wonder he doesn't write his own scripts, she mused, he's extremely articulate. With immaculate manners he led her to the door, accepting her thanks for his time with modest smiles.

Caitlin was delighted. On her pad was a wealth of good material, and she knew the article would be a success. 'I appreciate all your help.' She beamed her farewell, but as she turned away Bryce hesitated.

'I should ask Alison to check that before you go ahead,' he said with a frown.

Caitlin nodded. 'I will.'

Over the next few days she happily sifted through the information he'd provided and wrote up the article. Alison was still absent, but she went ahead, pruning and polishing, until she was totally satisfied with the result. Privately she didn't consider Alison could have done much better, and when the columnist didn't return the following week Caitlin decided to show her work to the editor.

'This is good.' The editor flicked approving eyes over the pages and Caitlin thrilled with pride. 'Can't say I know anything at all about Bryce Cameron, I'm usually too busy to watch his series, but he's quite a wit, isn't he?' She laughed. 'I love this quote—"It's been my experience that sex objects never object."' She smiled at Caitlin over the top of her bifocals. 'You've done a fine job here, but give credit where it's due, your subject made it easy.'

She nodded agreement, Bryce deserved her gratitude.

'Go ahead with it,' the editor instructed.

Alison eventually struggled back to the office, pale and snuffly.

'I've been hearing glowing reports on your Bryce Cameron write-up, let's have a look.' The columnist wiped her nose on a damp handkerchief. 'How come you managed to wheedle so much info from him?'

'No idea,' Caitlin said, for she hadn't.

'Probably because you're young and pretty,' Alison sniffed. 'Hand over the proofs.'

She waited as the older woman read her work, smugly expecting praise. Instead Alison frowned when she reached the final sentence and started to re-read the article again.

'Sorry, Honeybun,' she sighed, 'but I'm afraid this can't be printed. Bryce has been taking you for a ride, over the hills and far away.'

Caitlin stared at her in astonishment. 'What do you mean?'

'You weren't interviewing Bryce at all. You were interviewing Slattery.'

She wrinkled her brow in question.

'See this description of the exercise programme he's supposed to follow?' Alison prodded a finger. 'I'm prepared to swear on a stack of bibles that Slattery said that in the last episode. I know Bryce is keen on fitness, but he's also a busy man. He'd never have so much time to spare on jogging around. He's not an athlete.' She peered at Caitlin. 'Didn't it strike you as being exaggerated?'

An icy hand squeezed her heart. 'No,' she said in a small voice, but even as she said it doubts began to crowd her mind.

'And there's this account of where he spends his free

time.' Alison quoted, ' "I fly down to my ocean-going yacht which is always anchored off Capri, waiting for my command." ' She smiled wryly. 'That definitely is Slattery. You must have seen that gorgeous yacht, Caitlin. Surely you've watched the series?'

'Yes,' she admitted, her stomach knotting with tension. 'But I thought perhaps he allowed the television company to film on his own boat.'

'Listen, Honeybun, Bryce may be rich, but he's not that rich. He could never afford to have a yacht cruising around doing nothing for ten months of the year when he's working.'

A trapdoor slammed above Caitlin's head.

'And all the wisecracks,' the columnist continued ruthlessly. 'I bet they're a direct steal from *Slattery* scripts past and present.'

The entire article was a catalogue of disaster, Caitlin realised, a void of despair replacing the heady glow of satisfaction.

'There'll have to be drastic rewriting.' Alison began to score out lines of typescript. 'Some of your descriptions we can retain, but the quotes which smack too much of *Slattery* must go.'

To keep herself from crying Caitlin bit at the fleshy inside of her lower lip until there was the taste of blood. She'd been so delighted, so proud of the article, but all the time it had been a sham.

'He's a bastard, isn't he?' Alison commented sympathetically, noticing the tears which threatened to brim over. 'Don't worry, we can straighten it all out. If there are too few words we can use more photographs, that'll please his fans.'

'I hate him,' Caitlin declared through gritted teeth.

Alison leaned across and patted her hand. 'I don't suppose he ever imagined the article would be printed,' she said, by way of justification.

'He did tell me to check with you before it was

published.' It was a grudging admission. 'And he said if I needed more information to contact his agent.'

'Then that's what we must do.' Briskly Alison reached for the telephone and asked the switchboard for the number. As she waited she sat back in her chair, tapping her teeth with a pencil. 'I wonder why he did it?' she mused. 'Perhaps he was having a joke with you.'

The telephone rang out. As the columnist spoke, Caitlin's mind raced furiously. He's despicable, a cold calculating monster, she thought. He was baiting me and I fell for it. Her face flamed with shame as she remembered how grateful she'd felt towards him.

'Thank you, Mr Cameron,' she had said, and he had accepted her thanks so graciously, the swine.

Alison replaced the receiver. 'It seems Bryce was well aware he'd been a naughty boy. He told his agent I'd be calling. He's left some information, they're sending it round today.' She smiled at the girl's woebegone expression. 'Cheer up, it's not the end of the world.'

'If you'd been ill much longer the article would have been published,' Caitlin burst out. 'It would have been dreadful. I would have been forced to give in my resignation, and go home in disgrace. My career in journalism would have been finished.'

The older woman made comforting noises. 'But it never happened,' she pointed out. 'Everything will end happily, you'll see.'

She was right. The article was a success, despite being grossly rewritten using the information received from Bryce's agent. Caitlin and Alison worked on it together, spending long hours at the office when everyone else had gone home.

When it was finally completed Caitlin clenched her fists. 'I hope I never see that dreadful man again,' she declared, her eyes burning feverishly.

'He's taught you something,' Alison commented. 'Check your information, never believe all you're told.'

'I certainly won't,' she retorted with feeling.

But she had seen Bryce again—regularly every Tuesday evening. When the new *Slattery* series was shown Caitlin found herself sitting, with morbid fascination, before the television set. It was impossible to keep away. She had a compulsion to discover the worst, and it was all there—the smooth references to the yacht, the sexy quips, the casual humorous asides. Every time he opened his mouth to speak, she cringed. She studied the handsome face in detail, absorbing the way his full mouth curved into a smile, the arrogant glare when he was annoyed, the lift of a brow which could indicate everything, or nothing. When he uttered words which she recognised his eyes sparkled with devilment, a devilment which seemed to be directed only at her, making Caitlin feel sick inside.

It was a relief when the series ended and she was released from her self-inflicted torture. Now there were no more evenings with Joelle breathing open admiration, while she quivered with fury. To hell with Bryce Cameron, she thought savagely, and to hell with Slattery!

Eventually her bruised feelings healed. Memories of Bryce evaporated beneath a heavy and interesting workload, and as months passed, Caitlin became more experienced. Her outlook was poised and sharper, and Matthew was no longer the saviour he had originally seemed. Now she could stand on her own two feet, and his loyal attendance ceased to flood her with gratitude. But he was always there, waiting patiently for her to return to his arms when spasmodic relationships with other young men had run their course. And return to him she did, though she could never quite decide why.

Because Matthew knew she enjoyed the theatre, he had bought tickets for a smash-hit comedy. Caitlin waited for him in the foyer, inspecting her watch with increasing frequency, for it was unusual for Matthew to be late. She wriggled her toes in her tight shoes and watched the crowds pushing past her with interest. There were shrill greetings and bursts of laughter as rendezvous were kept. Smartly dressed women in smoking suits and velvet capes hurried by with debonair escorts, and she smiled, happy to be part of the London scene. In her white fur jacket she knew she looked good. The soft fur flattered her smooth complexion and rich hair, and several men gave her the eye as she waited. Again she consulted her watch. The first bell would ring soon. Where was Matthew? She was wondering if she should telephone his flat when possessive fingers gripped her shoulder and a low voice whispered into her ear.

'I believe I owe you an apology.'

The husky Scots accent was instantly recognisable, and she pivoted to glare into laughing eyes. It was impossible to ignore the raw maleness of the man beneath the tailored cut of an expensive charcoal-grey suit, and she stiffened.

Without a word his eyes travelled from the top of her glossy head to the pointed toes of her high-heeled shoes, lingering insolently over the fur jacket and tight suede trousers. His mouth curved into a smile of approval.

'I suppose you thought tricking me was very amusing,' she snapped before he could speak. His brows arched in genuine surprise at her attack, then he flashed a thousand-watt smile which would have turned sour milk into fresh cream. Several women faltered in their steps as they passed by, hoping to bask in the fringe of his benevolence.

'Forgive me,' he coaxed.

Caitlin was unimpressed. 'You are a conniving bastard, Mr Cameron,' she hissed through her teeth.

Bryce looked mortally offended. 'Come on, Sunshine, I'm sure once you returned to your office you quickly realised I was teasing.' He stopped and narrowed his eyes. 'Or did you?'

She looked away.

'Oh no,' he said, starting to laugh. 'Don't tell me you fell for it?'

There was a layer of ice in the hazel eyes which scraped over him. Abruptly his laughter faded, and he lifted his fingertips to touch her cheek. 'I'm sorry. I never dreamed you'd believe it all. You caught me on a bad day. I was furious at being mistaken for Slattery.'

She pushed his hand away, aware of a petulant blonde folding her arms in the background.

'There's no need for apology, Mr Cameron.' Her voice was stone cold. 'You gave me a valuable lesson; never to trust anyone, especially actors.'

'Ouch.' He gave a mock flinch. 'Don't tell me I'm responsible for the hard-headed young woman who stands before me?'

'I'm not hard-headed,' she retorted, 'but I am disillusioned, thanks to you.'

'Don't be too harsh,' he pleaded, bending his head and glancing at her through his lashes, his eyes wide and beguiling.

Caitlin curled her fingers to keep from thumping him. The approach was so familiar. She'd seen it a thousand times on the television. It was the look he reserved to seduce the *Slattery* women. The dark eyes would flash, he'd murmur his desire, and whisk them up into his arms.

'Save the sexy glances,' she taunted.

Bryce took a deep breath and pushed his hands into his trouser pockets. The suave play-acting was over. His irritation was plain to detect in the hard clench of his jaw. Caitlin felt a little surge of satisfaction. There was a temptation to rile him further, but the crowds parted and a man appeared before them, panting heavily. Nonplussed for a moment, Caitlin stared at him then realised it was Matthew.

'Sorry I'm late,' he gasped, thrusting a large box of chocolates into her hands. 'The taxi had a flat tyre. I had to walk miles before I could find another.' His face was flushed and his hair tousled across his forehead. He was not at all like the immaculate, well-organised Matthew.

Suddenly he became aware of Bryce's glowering presence and his features split into a wide smile. 'So pleased to meet you,' he gushed, grabbing Bryce's hand and pumping it up and down. 'I love the series. I think you're a great actor.'

'It's a relief to know somebody does.' Bryce threw Caitlin a look of disgust.

'You're fantastic, fantastic,' Matthew assured him. 'I never miss an episode.'

Peevishly Caitlin dug him in the ribs. 'We must go in.'

'What? Yes. Of course.' The idiot's grin still shone over Bryce. 'Nice to have met you, Mr Cameron. Caitlin didn't tell me you are one of her friends.'

Bryce turned on his heel and walked back to the blonde. 'I'm not,' he said over his shoulder.

CHAPTER THREE

SMUG delight bubbled through her when she awoke and realised today was the day she would have her revenge on Bryce Cameron. The prospect had a certain piquancy, and Caitlin hummed to herself as she bathed and shampooed her hair. So Bryce approved of the cascade of chestnut curls, did he? With vigorous strokes she brushed her hair until it clouded around her shoulders like a gleaming curtain. The hand which applied her make-up was rock steady. She had become skilled at the art of emphasising her hazel eyes without the effort appearing too extreme. She fingertipped muted cinnamon shadow on to her lids, and added a paler shadow to the bone. Two thin coats of mascara were carefully brushed on to her naturally thick lashes, and then a caress of blusher was stroked on to the high cheekbones. Lip-gloss completed the routine. The final result was satisfying. The *ingénue* who had plastered on lipstick and heavy black goo in an attempt to appear older had long since been overtaken by a confident young woman, certain of her own attraction.

With deft hands she took a cream suede suit from the hanger. After fastening the clip of the skirt at her slender waist, she slipped into a silky sleeveless top in pale avocado-green. The colour contrasted with the darkness of her hair and eyes, and the material clung softly to her womanly curves. Caitlin smoothed the skirt down over her hips and added an edge to edge jacket. Tiny gold studs were fitted into her ears, and a slender gold chain was clasped around her neck. Sling-back sandals and matching clutch bag completed the outfit. After a quick mist of expensive French perfume, a gift from Matthew, and another quick twirl of the styling brush, she was ready. A glance in the mirror assured her that this time Bryce would be impressed. Now she was an equal.

Her smile was mischievous. He had remarked on how much she had changed, but he had yet to realise how drastically. She fully intended to manipulate him as competently as he had manipulated her. Now she possessed the confidence to deal with the rampant sexuality which he switched on and off like an electric fire. Over the intervening months she'd had ample experience of good-looking men like Bryce, and this time Caitlin Saunders would not allow herself to become even warmed by his appeal, let alone singed.

'My word, you're looking smart,' her uncle said approvingly when he joined her at the breakfast table.

'You look very trendy yourself,' she smiled as he picked up the morning paper. 'Is that a new sweater?'

Desmond glanced down bashfully at the brightly patterned Fair Isle. 'Elsie knitted it for me.'

'It's beautiful.'

'Do you think so?' he asked, stroking the wool with admiring fingers.

'A labour of love,' Caitlin teased. 'It must have taken her weeks to knit, it looks very complicated.'

'It is.' He laid down the newspaper. 'You're seeing that Cameron chap today, Cait,' he began uncertainly. 'Couldn't you persuade him to pop round for a cup of tea while Elsie's here? She watches all his programmes.'

Caitlin gave a sigh. 'I'm sorry, Uncle Desmond, but no.'

He looked so crestfallen that she was immediately contrite. 'Look, suppose I ask him for a signed photograph? Will that please her?'

Desmond cheered up. 'She'd be thrilled to bits.'

Dark clouds were filling the sky as Caitlin wiped up the breakfast pots and she eyed them with dismay. It was too far to walk to the village in heavy rain. If she arrived to interview Bryce wet and bedraggled, she would be at a disadvantage, and today she needed all the points to be on her side. Desmond noticed her frown.

'I'll run you to the King's Head in the car,' he offered, flexing his arms and fingers experimentally. 'It's high time I was back behind the steering wheel.'

'Do you think that's wise?' Her question was tinged with doubt.

'The doctor said I could drive whenever I felt fit enough, and today I do. I'm anxious to get the car on the move again, standing for so long hasn't done the engine any good. In any case, I know you don't trust it. If we leave straight away I'll be back home again in time for Elsie's arrival.'

Although it was much too early, Caitlin gratefully accepted the lift. Her uncle dropped her outside the hotel just as the first rain drops were beginning to fall.

'Could you ask that Cameron fellow to run you back home?' he queried, glancing up at the grey sky with a frown.

Suspiciously Caitlin narrowed her eyes. 'Is this some trick to get him to meet Mrs Richards?'

'No, no.' He gave a hasty assurance. 'Actually now that I'm back in the driver's seat again I thought Elsie and I might run over to that market garden near Matlock. She's been itching to buy some geranium plants for ages. I can't guarantee to be able to collect you, because I don't know what time we'll be back.'

Caitlin straightened up and smiled. 'Don't worry about me, I'll make my own way home. Enjoy yourselves.'

She watched as the Ford chugged steadily away on to the High Street. The gleaming Maserati was parked outside the front entrance to the hotel. Bryce was around somewhere, so presumably it wouldn't matter that she was half an hour early. Tightening her fingers around her clutch bag, she strode determinedly forward.

The drone of a vacuum cleaner in the far distance was the only indication of life as she crossed the thick patterned carpet of the entrance hall. Nine-thirty was a hiatus. Residential guests would have already finished breakfast, and folk in search of morning coffee would traipse in later, around eleven. With the flat of her hand she hit the shining brass bell on the reception counter and waited. No response. After a few moments she slammed down on the bell again, but only the hum of the distant machine broke the silence. The bar, which stretched along one side of the oak-beamed hall, was deserted, and the door to the restaurant firmly shut.

Caitlin inspected several corridors which led to the kitchens and other sundry rooms, but they were silent and empty. Should she commandeer the register which lay open on the reception desk and discover the number of Bryce Cameron's room for herself? She was pondering on this possibility when a peal of feminine laughter came from the rear of the building. With head on one side she tentatively followed the direction of the sound along a shadowy corridor. The laughter came again, followed by a deep masculine chuckle. Perhaps Bryce was already entertaining his fans. Doubtless a regular slug of female adoration was necessary to keep him functioning.

When she reached a heavy wooden door labelled 'Lounge' Caitlin turned the handle. There was no sign of Bryce, but she recognised the voluptuous figure of Eleanor Halbert reclining among comfortable cushions on a chintz sofa. The actress was engrossed in conversation with a swarthy, bald-headed man in his fifties. He lolled by the French windows, speaking rapidly, flashing grandiose gestures and provoking more peals of laughter. Caitlin gave a small cough and walked forward. 'Excuse me, I'm looking for Mr Cameron. Please could you tell me where he is?'

Eleanor smiled and looked at her watch. 'I imagine he'll still be out jogging. Our Bryce is something of a fitness addict.'

The man by the window gave a grunt of disapproval which the actress calmly ignored.

'Have you come up from the city?' Her blue eyes shrewdly assessed the fashionable pale suede suit. 'Are you a friend?'

There was a derisive grunt from the window.

Caitlin flushed at the innuendo in the sound. 'Certainly not.' Her retort was crisp. She was damned if she was going to be classified as one of his women.

Eleanor arched carefully contoured brows. 'I didn't mean to pry, but I presume you're not from around here?'

'I represent the *Bugle*, the local newspaper,' she explained. 'At present I'm working for them on a freelance basis. Normally I am based in London.'

'Ah.' There was a sigh of satisfaction as though the statement revealed all the actress had suspected. 'Have a seat.' She patted the sofa. 'As far as I can remember the jogging ends around now. I should allow Bryce five minutes before you go up. He's in room number seven.' With a bright smile she turned to the bald-headed man. 'He wears me out with all his energy.'

A third grunt. As politeness did not appear to be his forte, Caitlin decided to ignore him. She sat down on the sofa, smiling at the woman beside her.

'I'm Caitlin Saunders.'

'And I'm Eleanor Halbert, and the moody individual over there is Frank Stern. He's directing the current episode of *Slattery*.' She shook an admonishing finger. 'Don't be sulky, Frank.' She laughed. 'It would do you good to take more exercise. You're developing a tummy. Now come over here and try to be friendly.'

The man obeyed her teasing command, forcing a reluctant smile as he sat down opposite. There was an awkward silence. Caitlin sensed undercurrents in the atmosphere.

'When do you start filming?' she asked, to fill the gap.

'Sunday,' Eleanor supplied. 'We're rehearsing at present, but the cameras roll in earnest next week.'

'I want to get the car chase out of the way first,' Frank intervened unexpectedly. He cast a glance at the misty rain swirling outside the window. 'It all depends on the blasted weather. Typical England! One minute it's freezing, then it pours down, and later the sun comes out. If we're lucky enough to have a fine day we should film the car sequence in a morning. Bryce has prepared everything in detail. All we need now are a couple of old cars to wreck.' He drew a hand across his head. 'And a police cordon to control the crowds.'

Caitlin grinned. 'That will be difficult. There's only a sergeant and one constable at the village police station.'

'Then they'll have to manage. It's damned expensive if we have to bring in a security firm,' he grumbled. 'Spectators are a pain in the neck. You've no idea of the trouble we have. I've been forced to scrap miles of film in the past because some snotty-nosed schoolboy popped up his head in the middle of a scene. It's difficult to maintain the illusion of Russian spy country with kids riding around on bikes making vee signs at the cameras.'

The two women laughed.

'And having a heart-throb like Bryce around doesn't help any,' he continued glumly. 'It's not only kids who follow the film crew, it's women as well.'

'Bryce would charm the pants off anyone.' Eleanor was serene.

'And frequently does.' Frank gave a mirthless bark, fixing the actress with melancholy eyes before turning

to glower out again at the rain. There was another
awkward pause. Quickly Caitlin rose.

'I'll go and see if Mr Cameron is ready.'

'Turn left at the top of the stairs,' the actress
instructed with a smile, 'and it's the room at the end of
the corridor.'

There was still no sign of life as Caitlin trekked back
across the entrance hall and mounted the staircase.
When she reached room number seven she took a deep
breath and knocked briskly.

'Come in.' The reply was strangled.

Her eyes grew round as copper coins when she saw
Bryce. He was lying flat out on the carpet doing press-
ups, counting on the intake of breath as he raised and
lowered himself. The heavy forearms tightened and
slackened as his body rose and fell. His eyebrows lifted
in surprise at her sudden entrance, but his pace was
relentless.

'Twenty more,' he gasped between numbers. Caitlin
folded her arms and leant back against the closed door,
viewing him dispassionately. Again he was half naked,
but this time, in place of tight jeans, he was clad in the
trousers of his black velour track suit. She gave a
cursory glance at the wide shoulders and sighed in
exasperation. It was as though he had deliberately
planned to provoke her by flaunting his vibrant
masculinity, but he didn't know she was coming. Her
brow puckered. Or did he? Had Maurice blunted her
weapon of surprise by passing on her identity?

But surely Bryce wouldn't have begun his play-acting
so early, she wasn't due for another twenty minutes.
Grudgingly she accepted that the display of male
strength was not for her entertainment only, it was a
regular work-out. Diverting her gaze from the rhythmic
body, she surveyed the room. The left-hand side had
been furnished as a lounge, complete with armchairs,
sofa, writing desk and television. To the right was a

king-size bed, old-fashioned mahogany wardrobe and dressing table, and beyond an open door which revealed a bathroom tiled in muted shades of green.

'Phew!' Bryce collapsed in a heap on the floor, then, after a split second, jumped to his feet and began to towel away rivulets of perspiration which coursed down the rippling muscles.

'Have you come to apologise?' A sardonic brow arched in question. 'That dog of yours could have caused a nasty accident, to the car and to me.' The thick white towel rubbed roughly along one glistening arm. 'Hurry up, don't waste time.' His manner was brusque, making her swallow hard to beat down a rush of temper. Control of her emotions was vital. She wasn't about to blow her revenge by succumbing to anger.

'Are you in a rush?' she asked sweetly.

'Some old biddy's coming from the local paper to interview me at ten,' he rasped out, his dark hairy chest still rising and falling from his exertion. 'I must shower and change before she arrives.'

Caitlin felt a glow of satisfaction. So he didn't know she would be writing the article! She had caught him unprepared.

'Why bother putting on any more clothes, Mr Cameron?' she purred. 'Don't you always meet the press half naked? Surely it's part of the image?' Scathing hazel eyes scoured across the smooth shoulders and flat midriff.

Bryce noticed her scrutiny and frowned. 'No,' he snapped.

Resting her hands lightly on her hips she tapped one toe reflectively. 'How many miles did you jog this morning—twenty?'

He flung the towel aside. 'Three,' he said tight-lipped. 'It looked like rain, and besides there were two bloody girls following me on motor scooters yelling obscene suggestions.' He gave a snort of such utter disgust that Caitlin laughed.

'I'm surprised you didn't respond,' she glinted. 'Sex objects never object.'

'Touché. You appear to have an answer for everything.'

'As you did, two years ago.'

He sighed heavily. 'For heaven's sake, I've already apologised for that. You caught me on the raw. You've no idea of the pressures which mount up when you have to live, day in, day out, with a character like Slattery.'

'I would have imagined it had its moments, Mr Cameron.'

He cast her a darkly furious look. 'And another thing, do you think you could stop calling me Mr Cameron? It makes me feel a thousand years old. I'm only thirty-three.'

'Do you still have your own teeth?' Caitlin's mouth lurched with amusement and he suddenly relaxed.

'Shall I bite you to prove it?' he grinned.

'No, thank you.' Hastily she pulled up the drawbridge. Humour must not distract her from her purpose. Bryce was proving relatively easy to handle when he was ill-tempered, but if she succumbed to that fatal charisma and began trading wisecracks and smiles, she was well aware she might end up in trouble. She must never forget that he wasn't to be trusted an inch.

With one fluid movement he sat on the edge of the bed and pulled her down beside him. It was a casual gesture, but she was too acutely aware of the male nakedness of his upper body to feel at ease. Lazily his look caressed her.

'You're gorgeous, Cait. I've never noticed before how beautiful your eyes are.' He leaned towards her. 'Like tawny pools. A man could drown in them.'

Hurriedly she lowered her lashes. The way he was inspecting her, as though he was seeing her for the first time, sent prickles of agitation pitter-pattering along her limbs.

'What would you like me to do for you?' he asked.

Caitlin frowned at the way he had phrased the question.

'Why should I want you to do anything for me?' She left the bed and walked away to the safe distance of the window, trying to ignore the intent dark eyes which followed her retreat. For retreat it was. The close proximity of such a ruggedly attractive man was tightening her as taut as a tripwire.

'Because everyone does,' he replied. 'When you become well known everyone wants a piece of the action. I have no illusions.'

'It works the other way round, too.' Her voice and her look were level. 'If you are a star you take what you want, no questions asked.'

'Perhaps.' His jaw tightened, stretching the thin white scar. He was irritated by her comment. She wondered if anyone told him the truth any more, probably he only heard what he wanted to hear.

'Actually, I do want something.' Unconsciously the pointed chin thrust upwards. 'Please could I have a signed photograph?'

Bryce gave a hoot of derision. 'Come on, Sunshine, what the hell do you want a photograph for? Are you going to pin it over your bed to give you sweet dreams?'

'It's not for me,' she explained hastily. 'It's for my uncle's daily help.'

He started to laugh. The colour mounted in her face as he rocked backwards and forwards on the bed, almost doubled up with laughter.

' 'Struth,' he spluttered, 'the things I'm asked to do! Are you sure your dog wouldn't like one, too? I could scribble a touching message—"With best wishes to Duke for a speedy recovery." How is he, by the way, any more problems with that paw?'

'None. He's fit and well,' Caitlin replied coldly.

He studied her unrelenting profile and struggled to regain his composure. 'You amaze me,' he crowed. 'Do you mean to say you've made a special visit, dressed in your Sunday best, merely to ask for a photograph for some charlady?'

Nervously she stroked the edge of her jacket. 'There's more to it than that,' she confessed.

Bryce left the bed and came towards her. 'You've decided I'm not such a bad guy after all.' His eyes sparked impudently. 'You want to show your appreciation in the usual way.'

'I do not.' The retort was hot. She knew exactly what he meant. The confident masculine sexuality was oozing from him as he stretched out a fingertip and gently traced the line of her temple and cheekbone.

'It's hardly a fate worse than death,' he taunted. 'Some have been known to enjoy it.'

'I've come to interview you.'

He looked puzzled and dropped his hand.

'I'm the old biddy from the *Bugle*,' she revealed, with a smug lift of her brow. 'I freelance for them. Maurice Gill asked if I would write about you.'

'So you wheedled your way into my room under false pretences!' he accused, his face darkening in furious comprehension.

'I did not!'

'You could have told me you were here on business,' he challenged.

'I didn't have much opportunity with you floundering around on the carpet like a grounded whale.'

'You love to cut me down to size, don't you?' he said wryly, his eyes glittering. Then the corner of his mouth twitched. 'I thought I looked like Michelangelo's David.'

The tip of her tongue protruded between her lips. 'A lump of old stone, you mean?'

'One of the wonders of the world was more what I had in mind.' Laughter simmered in his eyes as he waited for the next thrust.

'We all have our fantasies,' Caitlin rejoined, then she moved towards the sofa. 'I'll wait here while you change, Mr . . .' she hesitated, 'Bryce. Then we can start work.' She sat down and crossed her legs. Pad and pencil were taken out from her bag with brisk, businesslike movements. He surveyed her thoughtfully for a moment then, conceding defeat, disappeared into the bathroom.

Idly she doodled with her pencil as she waited. No notes were necessary. She knew exactly what she wanted, another spiel about the high life, but Bryce's this time, not Slattery's. That, too, must contain gaudy blondes, lavish parties, rice-paper-thin love affairs. She almost chuckled out loud with delight as she visualised her revenge. Bryce had said she loved to cut him down to size, and she'd do it so beautifully on paper.

Caitlin was still smiling to herself when he emerged, hair freshly shampooed and curling damply on to the collar of a chocolate-brown shirt. His tailored slacks were the colour of peat.

'What's so funny?' he demanded, sitting down beside her.

'Nothing.'

His dark eyes were wary. 'You're different. In some ways it's a vast improvement,' his gaze slid down her body as if to confirm his point, 'but in other ways I'm not so sure.'

'You won't trick me this time.'

'I won't try,' he assured her solemnly. He fingered the scar on his jaw. 'Before we start I'd like to explain something, off the record.'

Caitlin set aside the pad and pencil. 'Go ahead.'

'*Slattery* has been good to me,' he started, 'and I know I shouldn't complain, but there are days when I think I'll throw up if anyone mentions the name again. I don't just act him, I have to be him. Our personalities are intermingled in the public eye. I recognise that it's partly my own fault. When the series first started I threw myself into it, and the publicity angle, with a vengeance, then when I wanted to retreat I couldn't, I was already branded.'

'But he's only a character,' she pointed out.

He raised his eyes to the ceiling and gave a despairing snort. 'Oh yes? At first I was Bryce Cameron, the actor. Then it was Bryce Cameron who played Slattery. Now it's virtually become Slattery interpreted by Bryce Cameron.'

'Nobody's forcing you to play him. Why don't you stop if you hate the role so much?'

He stood up and paced across the carpet, hands deep in his pockets. 'I intend to. This episode in Derbyshire is the final one of the present series. After that there's a film, then . . .' A large hand sliced through the air. 'Then kaput.'

'Isn't another television run planned?' Caitlin enquired, wrinkling her brow. She was sure she'd read it somewhere.

'It's in the pipeline,' he confirmed with a scowl, 'but I intend to break my contract.'

'How long are you tied to it?'

'Two more years, it was five in all.'

She looked at him aghast. 'They'll sue if you try and renege now.'

'I'm well aware of that,' he said grimly. 'It'll cost me a packet, but I refuse to play damn Slattery for ever.'

'Why did you sign such a long-term agreement?' She was well aware television contracts were often on an annual basis.

'I needed security.' He gave a self-deprecating smile. 'I'd spent years playing juvenile leads with good crits and lousy money, so when this offer was first mooted I jumped in with both feet.' Irritably he rubbed the back of his neck. 'I know actors have a reputation for being erratic individuals who care little for a planned life, but not me. I've no intention of spending my old age struggling to make ends meet.' He turned to her despairingly. 'I hated never knowing where the next penny was coming from. The sheer impermanence of the acting game was getting me down. If *Slattery* hadn't come along when it did I'd have abandoned the theatre and gone into the motor business. At least that pays a regular wage.' His smile was lukewarm. 'I was becoming heartily sick of pizza and chips.'

'And now you're heartily sick of oysters?' she asked.

He gave her a swift glance. 'Yes,' he conceded.

'Aren't you afraid you'll always be identified with Slattery in the future?'

'Terrified,' he admitted, pulling his mouth into a downward curve. 'I wake up in the night wondering if he'll be an albatross around my neck.'

'Strong characters can be abandoned, though, given time and care,' she said slowly. 'It has been done before.'

'That's what I try and persuade myself.'

The journalist in Caitlin rose to the top. What a scoop his decision to quit *Slattery* would be!

'When are you intending to make the news public?'

There was a pause as Bryce weighed his words. 'Not for a while. I intend to finalise my plans carefully. I own some garages, employ over a hundred people, I don't intend to have them put at risk.' He returned to sit beside her. 'I shall complete the film, announce my decision, then try to avoid the media for a while.'

'And give the public a well-earned rest from your face?'

He chuckled. 'Lovely Cait, you have a delightful way of expressing yourself.' He reached across and twisted a glossy tendril of hair around his index finger, making

Caitlin's nerves leap with an awareness of him.

'How come I'm telling you all this?' he mused slowly.

As his fingers moved to caress the smooth plane of her cheek, she fought to resist the magnetism which was pulling her towards him. The tender touch of his fingertips was making her soft and pliable, like putty, she thought corrosively. It took an effort, but she shifted slightly away into her corner of the sofa. There was a flicker of amusement in his eyes as he, too, moved in the same direction.

Caitlin was determined to play it cool. 'What will you do without the Slattery girls?' she asked tartly.

'Find Cameron ones,' he murmured, concentrating on the silky angle of her jawbone. 'Would you like to be first in the queue?'

Poised to snap out some cutting remark she swung towards him, but the briskness of her movement disturbed her jacket and it fell open. The soft outline of her breasts was revealed beneath the clinging top.

There was a blur of desire in Bryce's eyes as he surveyed the full high curves.

'You're beautiful,' he said huskily.

Caitlin could feel her temperature soaring. She tried to remain in control of herself, but some other power, stronger than hers, took command. As though guided by invisible hands she and Bryce leant towards each other, and little by little they met in the middle. At first his lips merely brushed hers, softly, tentatively, but then he pushed his hand into the tumble of hair at the back of her head and his fingers tightened. His mouth was predatory as he forced her lips apart. He knew what he wanted. At first he took it greedily, but as the heat between them grew Caitlin found herself offering her mouth willingly to his kiss. He was no longer taking, it was a mutual offering. His breathing became low and deeply urgent as he slid his hands beneath the jacket to caress her shoulder-blades, his fingers kneading compulsively into her skin until she was aflame.

'You taste so fresh, Sunshine,' he muttered, his mouth leaving hers to blaze a trail down the curve of her throat. Caitlin gasped as she thrust her fingers into his thick hair, yielding her body to his. Men had kissed her before, but never like this. She was on fire, burning with a primitive need.

Bryce mumbled into her neck, then he slipped the jacket from her. Alarm bells began to ring in the foggy recesses of her mind. She struggled to keep her thoughts intact. This was wrong. Bryce was a low-down, conniving swine. She must not forget that. She hadn't come to be seduced, she'd come to teach him a lesson. Weakly she pushed at his chest with lifeless hands. It was as though she was in a dream. All resistance was futile. It was only as his fingers confidently captured her breast that she found the strength she needed and forced him from her.

'That's enough.' There was a taut pause. She knew the password, she would use it. 'Slattery,' she added in cold triumph.

With one supple movement he jerked himself upright.

'Bitch!' he ground out, his jaw working in anger. The sound of his ragged breathing filled the room. 'You're a calculating bitch!'

Unaccountably Caitlin felt ashamed of herself.

'You're not so bad at calculating yourself,' she retaliated, swallowing the urge to fling herself back into his arms and beg his forgiveness. Bryce balled his fists, clenching and unclenching the strong fingers as he fought to control the desire to hit her, or make love to her, he didn't know which. She read his thoughts. The leashed control was wavering and for one moment she thought he would strike out. Automatically she flinched, and Bryce gave a scornful laugh.

'I don't hit women. Slattery does, but not me.'

Caitlin retrieved her jacket and flung it around her shoulders. With trembling hands she thrust the pad into her clutch bag and headed for the door.

Bryce rocked indolently on his heels, smoothing down a thick sideburn. 'Aren't you forgetting something?' he drawled, as her hand closed around the doorknob.

'What?'

'The interview.'

'Oh.' Caitlin was flustered. Surely there was no chance of an interview now?

'Mr Gill will be very disappointed if you report back empty-handed,' Bryce said calmly. 'I'll spare you half an hour, then we're quits. Right?'

She hesitated, chewing her lip.

He spelt out the proposition. 'I'll allow you this interview despite *your* bad behaviour in payment for the last interview and *my* bad behaviour.'

Caitlin frowned. In her opinion she hadn't behaved badly. He had deserved to be slapped down. Suddenly she was too confused to argue. The matter could rest.

'And then we call a truce,' Bryce continued. 'We're back to square one.' He walked over to the desk and scrawled his signature on a photograph. 'Don't forget this,' he said, handing it to her. 'Do you agree that we're even?'

'Okay,' she said in a low voice.

Primly she returned to the sofa and took out her pad. The interview was subdued this time. The questions were answered frankly, but there were no spicy comments, no anecdotes concerning exotic tropical islands, no mention of fast women, fast cars and a breathtaking lifestyle. Instead he concentrated on the dangers involved in filming the stunts, the marketing of the *Slattery* series abroad, the restrictions of being constantly in the public eye.

Caitlin began to smoulder with exasperation. The

information he was giving her was not capable of producing the kind of article she had in mind. Hopefully she made several jokey references to the girls who slipped in and out of the series and their underwear, but he contemptuously ignored them.

'What about hobbies?' she asked, arching a saucy brow. The stern look in his dark eyes shrivelled her.

'Listening to Mozart, fiddling with old cars, messing about in boats—small boats,' he said firmly. 'Don't look so disbelieving. I'm sorry if it isn't what you had in mind, but it's what I enjoy.'

It was difficult to hide her disappointment, but how could she possibly poke fun at those innocent activities?

'And how's your sex life?' Her voice was brisk to quell the uneven beating of her heart. He eyed her with open scorn.

'You want a direct quote?'

Caitlin gave a little nod. She was not feeling very pleased with herself. The brash line of questioning jarred with the man before her. This Bryce Cameron was not the voluble extrovert she had met before. But then it had been Slattery, hadn't it?

'Write this down,' he instructed. 'The woman who has most recently aroused me has tawny-coloured eyes, a tantalising body, and is called Caitlin Saunders.' He thrust his hands in his pockets and turned his back on her to look out at the pouring rain. She glared at the wide set of his shoulders.

'Oh, and add this,' he threw at her. 'She promises to be a passionate lover.'

Caitlin bit down hard on her lip. 'You swine,' she muttered, the colour flaring hotly in her face.

'You wanted a quote about my sex life,' he tossed casually, 'and you damn well had one. If you'd like to strip and come to bed with me I can give you further copy.'

Furiously she flung herself towards the door.

'And another thing,' a cool voice informed her. 'I want to read that article before it's printed.'

The pointed chin jutted defiantly. 'Don't you trust me?'

'Not one little bit, Sunshine. Not one little bit.'

CHAPTER FOUR

THE splash of rain was cold on her burning cheeks. Caitlin stood, chest heaving, on the steps of the King's Head. She had hurtled from Bryce's room and out towards the street as though jet-propelled and was now startled to find herself alone, not quite knowing what to do next. The adrenaline which had given impetus to her flight was stemmed. Quickly she assembled her shattered thoughts. There was no point trudging back to the cottage in the pouring rain, she'd be reduced to a wet rag within minutes. It made far more sense to visit the *Bugle*'s offices for a while, and hope the weather would brighten.

With determined steps she made her way along the High Street, avoiding puddles and hamfisted shoppers wielding umbrellas. She would make a start on the write-up while it was fresh in her mind. Caitlin made a moue of irritation. It was all too fresh, especially the memory of Bryce's mouth on hers and the eager way she had responded. Furiously persuading herself away from such thoughts she concentrated on the article. How would it be angled? She hadn't a clue. Everything Bryce had told her was so low key. It would be incongruous to align a photograph of him sprawled in the magnificent Maserati with a comment on his delight at fixing the broken down engines of old cars. Who could imagine the immaculate millionaire detective with oil smeared on his chin and black fingernails!

If only she could announce his decision to quit *Slattery*, now that really would make a scoop. She wondered if she should telephone Alison and give her a hint, confidentially. Her tongue clicked in exasperation.

No, that was unfair. Bryce had told her his plans off the record, and she could not break his confidence. It would be unprofessional and immoral. She had always been strictly honest in her dealings with celebrities, and had no intention of breaking her code now. She would just make the best of the information she had, but how could she use the facts he'd given her? Running her fingers through her hair in frustration, she decided that he'd done it deliberately. He had played her at her own game, and damn him, he had won again.

Caitlin ran up the rickety steps to the newspaper offices feeling furious with herself. She couldn't work out yet what had happened, but one thing was certain, Bryce had seen through her scheming and forced her to take another direction by deliberately feeding her facts which suited his strategy.

'How did it go?' Maurice asked as she flung herself down in a chair before him.

She shook raindrops from her collar. 'Okay.'

'What did he tell you about his love life?' The editor gave a gurgle of anticipation.

'Nothing.' She refused to comment further.

For a moment he looked disappointed, then his face cleared. 'Perhaps it's just as well. I've been speaking to Sir Quentin. It appears Bryce Cameron has donated a car to be raffled for charity at the fête.'

Her brows soared.

'Not the Maserati,' Maurice said hastily. 'He's arranged a deal between a local dealer and one of the garages he owns in Scotland. He's providing a family saloon. Apparently sometimes he allows his name to be used to raise money for good causes, with overwhelming success.'

He clasped his hands behind his head and leant back. 'It makes a change to find someone like him using his fame for a constructive purpose. Did he tell you about it?'

'No,' she confessed with a grimace. She had slipped up there. All the facts about Bryce should have been at her fingertips, but obviously they weren't. He was a surprising man.

'In view of his generosity, I feel we should give him the common touch,' Maurice continued. 'We can't rabbit away about his jet-set lifestyle, and then reveal he's opening the village fête and supporting local charities, the two don't tie in.'

It was impossible to deny the reluctant surge of relief. 'Most of what he told me will suit,' she nodded. 'He's quite normal, really.'

'I don't suppose the poor chap can help looking like God's gift to women,' the editor said generously. 'Why don't you pop back to the King's Head now and ask him about this car he's donating? You could discover some details about his other charity interests too.'

Caitlin swallowed hard. There was no way she was returning to the lion's den. She desperately needed time to regain her composure and analyse her feelings about Bryce.

'I'll telephone,' she suggested. It was by far the lesser of the two evils.

'Use my office.' Maurice sauntered to the door of his cubicle. 'I must have a word with young Paul about tomorrow's fête. He's preparing a list of events, and splitting them between the two of you. I'll check if your half is ready.'

With a shaking finger she dialled the number and asked for Bryce's room. When the richness of his Scots burr sounded in her ear, her throat seized up.

'Caitlin here,' she croaked.

'Oh yes?' His voice was coldly formal.

'Could you tell me something about the car you're donating to the fête, and your other charity work?' It was hard to say, but after an infinitesimal pause she added, 'Please,' as she struggled to tread the fine line between independence and grovelling. She was sickeningly aware in which direction her foot was slipping.

'You didn't do your homework thoroughly, did you?'

She fought the temptation to blow a raspberry down the receiver.

'No,' she agreed meekly.

'And you're supposed to be the great professional,' he taunted.

Caitlin stuck out her tongue at the telephone.

'Will you be at the fête tomorrow?' he asked, when there was no reply.

'Yes.'

'Then I suggest you come and see me there.' He snapped down the phone, leaving Caitlin foolishly staring at the instrument in her hand. Maurice poked his head round the door.

'Everything organised?'

She rattled off what Bryce had suggested. Suggested? more like ordered.

'Now I'll make a start on the writing,' she said, rising to her feet.

The editor peered out at the rain. 'I'll run you home when you've finished, lass. It looks as though it's going to pour down all day. Let's hope it clears by tomorrow. Sir Quentin will be livid if it's wet two years on the trot for that fête of his.'

Caitlin worked hard. It was a relief to have something constructive to occupy her mind, and the discipline of writing kept her thoughts from sidetracking too wildly on to images of Bryce as a living, breathing, physical man. On paper he was safely pinned down. There he became merely a personality, though not the personality she had presumed him to be. The charisma was still present, but it was deeper, more sincere and definitely more appealing. She poked her pencil into the chestnut hair above her ear and reread what she had written. Was Bryce still acting, or was the character he had revealed today the true man? Perhaps he had merely abandoned the svelte playboy for the trusty pillar of society. She sighed. He'd tricked her once. She was unhappily aware that perhaps he'd tricked her again.

The familiar blare of the introduction to 'News at Ten' sounded in her ears, and Caitlin lifted the two empty mugs from the coffee table. 'I'll rinse these, and then go to bed,' she said wearily, making her way towards the kitchen.

'So early!' Her uncle shifted his eyes from the television screen in surprise.

'I'm tired.' Tired of thinking about Bryce, she admitted to herself. The entire evening's programmes had passed blindly before her eyes, and she couldn't recall a single item. I'm being ridiculous, she scolded herself, but even when she was undressed and in bed, the vivid memory of the feel and taste of him continued to revolve endlessly in her brain. Why should he disturb her so much? Other men had aroused her before, but never with such devastating effect. She remembered his words, that she promised to be a passionate lover. But she would never succumb to his charms. 'I shan't be one in a long line of girls,' she whispered.

When the telephone rang, shattering the peace of the night, she was still tossing and turning, unable to rest. Without pausing to collect her robe, she ran barefoot down the stairs in an attempt to lift the receiver before the noise disturbed her sleeping uncle.

'Hi, Cait, it's me, Joelle.' Disco music blared down the phone, filling the silent hallway with raucous gaiety. It was a totally alien sound. Caitlin peered through the darkness at the grandfather clock in the corner.

'It's after midnight,' she accused with a yawn.

Her cousin giggled. 'I'd forgotten you pull down the blinds at nine o'clock up there in the sticks. I'm ringing to tell you I shall be popping up to see Daddy for a few days.'

'Why?' Her voice was cautious.

The reply came smoothly, too smoothly. 'It's ages since I've seen him. I miss the dear old thing.'

Suspiciously Caitlin waited for more.

'I've studied the timetable,' Joelle announced. 'There's a train early Sunday morning. I'm short of cash, so I can't afford a taxi. I'll take the bus, it arrives in the village at noon. Will you tell Daddy to meet me in the car? I'll be laden down with luggage.'

'He'll be there,' she promised. Like everyone else Desmond was expected to fall in with Joelle's plans, this time in the capacity of porter. The fact that he was recovering from a stroke had been discounted. Suddenly everything clicked into place.

'You've heard about *Slattery*,' Caitlin said flatly.

'Yes.' Joelle never bothered to lie when she was cornered. 'I thought if I made my presence known I might manage to grab a part in the film.'

'Hope springs eternal!' The dry comment was a little unkind, but Caitlin was unable to resist it. The fact that Uncle Desmond came second to Slattery rankled.

Joelle giggled again. She sounded tipsy. 'Have you seen Bryce Cameron around?'

'Yes.'

'Is he still gorgeous?'

'If you like that kind of thing.' The words slashed irritably through the darkness.

'Who doesn't!'

Who doesn't indeed, Caitlin thought. She was merely feeling the way a hundred other women had felt after contact with Bryce. What a cliché! She gave out a sharp breath of self-disgust. Joelle heard her sigh and interpreted it as impatience.

'I'm sorry, did I wake you?' The dilatory apology fell on deaf ears.

'I'll make up the bed. Your father will be pleased to hear that you're coming.'

There was a babble of intoxicated conversation from Joelle, further giggles and a trill of goodbye. Slowly Caitlin crawled back into bed. Joelle was a typical Slattery blonde, so doubtless Bryce would turn his attentions to her. She yanked the blankets over her head. Why did the prospect of Joelle and Bryce together make her want to run away and howl like an animal in pain?

'Sir Quentin's prayers have been answered,' Desmond announced as Caitlin came down to breakfast the following morning. He pushed aside the blue and white gingham curtains. 'Look at that sunshine.'

She joined him at the window. The dull grey skies had been painted China-blue, with not a cloud in sight.

'Good job you brought something light to wear,' her uncle continued, his glance taking in her sleeveless cotton dress. 'It's going to be warm. You can smell it in the air.' Flinging wide the window he took several deep breaths. 'Makes you feel good to be alive.'

Caitlin notched the last hole in her wide waist-hugging belt and slipped the end through the loop. Her dress was a rust-coloured button-through, with full skirt and ruffled jabot neckline. As she adjusted golden hoops in her ears she smiled. Her uncle was right, it *did* feel good to be alive. The bright sunshine was rapidly stilling the throb of tension in her temples, for sleep had proved elusive. Fortunately the only indication of her lack of rest was faint smudges beneath her eyes, and she had carefully drawn attention away from these by the skilful use of sorrel-tinted shadow on her lids, and a soft shade of amber lip-gloss.

When the dishes had been dried and stacked away, Desmond inspected his watch. 'Are you ready? I told Elsie we'd pick her up about eleven.'

'Shall I make a picnic?' Caitlin asked. 'Isn't the fête an all-day event?'

'It is,' he smiled, 'but we can buy something to eat there. One of the large reception rooms at Greaves Court is fitted out as a snack bar for the day. They serve delicious lunches and afternoon teas.' Again he consulted his watch. 'I know we're on the early side, but shall we go? I want some leeway in case the car doesn't start easily. I don't want to keep Elsie waiting.'

Caitlin grabbed her bag from the hall table as he hurried her outside and into the car. Determination set his face as he carefully turned the ignition key. To their joint amazement the Ford chugged over first time, steadying off into a robust hum as he pressed down on the accelerator. They both looked at each other and laughed.

Although they were far too early, Mrs Richards came out on to her doorstep the minute they drew up, smartly attired in matching coat and dress of turquoise Crimplene, and a white straw hat trimmed with daisies.

'Lovely to see you again,' she bubbled delightedly as though it had been weeks, and not the previous day, when they had last met. Desmond leapt out to greet her, fussing around with such tender loving care that Caitlin was forced to smother a grin. The couple treated each other with the bashful delight of young lovers, and the entire journey to Greaves Court was rich with pleasantries and compliments which they traded incessantly between them.

The main drive was already thick with traffic, and they were forced to queue for several minutes before being directed on to the field which had been designated as a car park for the day. The Ford rattled over the rough grass so noisily that Caitlin would not have been surprised if it had suddenly fallen apart like a trick taxi in a comedy routine.

'Suppose we all meet up at the car park around four?'

Desmond suggested, as they joined the crowds making
their way towards the showground and collection of
marquees erected on the wide lawns. From the corner
of her eye Caitlin saw him squeeze Mrs Richards' arm.

'Fine. I'll go and find Paul,' she said, her pace
quickening. The old couple were too engrossed,
whispering to each other, to notice her departure and
she grinned. It was a relief that she would be too busy
to spend the day playing gooseberry to a pair of love-
struck sixty-year-olds.

Greaves Court was an imposing manor house built
towards the end of the last century. A flight of steps led
to a wide porch, supported by four Grecian-style
pillars, and two wings spread solidly to east and west of
the main body of the building. Large casement windows
overlooked the lawns which were rapidly filling with
visitors dressed in gay summer clothes. To the left was
the showground, a vast green rectangle marked out by
restraining ropes, and surrounded by banks of red
plastic chairs. At one end was a wooden stage, colourfully
decorated with red, white and blue flags. On it were two
rows of seats, carefully positioned to accommodate
local dignitaries, and at the front was a podium with a
silver microphone.

Buying a programme from a Boy Scout, Caitlin
studied it carefully. The day promised to be a busy one.
In fifteen minutes' time Bryce was scheduled to open
the activities with a speech of welcome, and immediately
following him there would be dancing around the
Maypole erected in the centre of the showground, a
display by the local Morris dancers, children's fancy
dress parade, and a beautiful baby competition. After
lunch there was to be a mini gymkhana, and finally a
performance by the dog handling unit of the police
force. Displays of flowers, vegetables, home-baking and
handicrafts were housed in white marquees on the right-
hand side of the lawns. These would be judged and the

prizes, together with the winner of the car raffle, announced at the end of the afternoon. Roundabouts, swings, and a variety of games of chance, had been provided for the children.

Caitlin made her way past the sideshows, throwing a glance towards the dais where the car Bryce had gifted was displayed. It was a spanking bright yellow, gleaming in the sunshine. Some lucky person would leave the fête a delighted owner. The entire village appeared to have come along, determined to enjoy themselves. Toddlers ran around trailing coloured balloons, families relaxed on the grass, and the ice cream van was already attracting brisk trade. Paul was waiting by the First Aid tent.

'Great day,' he commented happily, looking up at the clear blue sky. 'All ready for the off?'

Caitlin nodded.

'Will you make a note of Bryce Cameron's speech?' the boy asked.

'Okay,' she agreed. She tossed back a strand of glossy hair. She would report his speech, discover the details of his charity interests and then make certain there was plenty of space between them.

Paul glanced round. 'Here he comes,' he announced, eyes wide.

Caitlin felt her pulses shudder, and break into a nervous gallop. As if by magic the crowds had parted to reveal an approaching group. Bryce was the focal point, taller by inches than any of the other men. His leashed energy was unmistakable in the smooth prowl of the long legs, the powerful glide of the broad shoulders. He wore a well cut beige suit and a dark shirt. Eleanor was hanging on to one arm, blonde hair drifting against his chest, while Frank marched sullenly by her side. Sir Quentin Greaves and his wife were on the other flank, while local officials milled around. They were followed by a motley group of children, autograph books clutched in sticky hands. The actor's progress through the villagers was like an emperor with his subjects, accepting their adulation and awe as no more than his due. The charisma flashed like a beacon, and Caitlin was fully aware that everyone was basking in its glow. More fans for the dream hero, she thought with a spasm of irritation.

Hastily she stepped behind Paul, hoping to avoid recognition, but with deadly accuracy the dark eyes snared hers. Bryce came to a full stop. As his entourage swirled haphazardly about him he excused himself from his host and strode towards her. Caitlin's lips curved into a tentative smile, but suddenly she froze. His eyes were stone hard. The easy friendliness bestowed on Sir Quentin and company had died, and as he reached her his face was tight with anger. His fury was reserved solely for her, and automatically her hand swept to her throat in fear. Only she was aware of the nerve jabbing in his jaw, the shoulders stiffening into a wall of steel, the controlled rise and fall of his chest. When he pulled her aside from Paul to speak, his voice was low and menacing.

'You bloody bitch!' he ground out.

Startled, Caitlin closed her eyes for a moment, blocking out his fury, then she braced herself. 'What's the matter?' she asked. Beyond his shoulder she was uncomfortably aware of an audience of curious bystanders.

'I thought I could trust you,' he snarled from the back of his throat. 'I'll speak to you later, just as soon as I've finished on stage. Wait here.' It was a bark of command.

Her senses battered by his angry assault, Caitlin stood rooted to the spot as he turned back to join the group. The charisma was flicked on again, and smiles dripped from him as he murmured something to Sir Quentin and made his way towards the stage.

'Masterful brute, isn't he?' Paul chuckled into her ear. She pressed her lips together, hoping the boy had not been able to hear the wrathful words.

A collective female sigh echoed over the showground as Sir Quentin finished his introduction and Bryce stepped forward. Caitlin recorded his words with a shaking pen, wryly noting that he successfully beguiled everyone with his easy blend of plain talking and wit. As soon as Bryce finished talking, Sir Quentin grabbed the microphone again, listing the day's events. Spinning on her heel, Caitlin moved away towards the marquees. The first breathless impact of Bryce's attack had lessened, and now her temper was beginning to spark. Did he imagine she was some dizzy starlet who could be ordered around? She tossed her head. No way did she intend to wait around in order to be insulted in public again.

'I'll check if the garden produce has been judged,' she announced, tucking the notebook into her bag.

'Too early yet,' Paul said, but she kept on walking, eyes travelling to right and left as she searched for a convenient place to hide.

'See you later,' she called over her shoulder, diving beneath a tarpaulin flap into blessed gloom. The marquee was empty. Competitors and judges alike had gone outside into the sunshine to listen to the speeches of welcome. Trestle tables held an orderly display of scrubbed vegetables. Caitlin pressed a hand to her burning brow. She was well aware that they had been the cynosure of all eyes when Bryce had confronted her, and had no intention of being placed in that embarrassing position again. The village was a hotbed of gossip. Any unusual behaviour was examined, prodded and discussed at length. Wise tactics now would be to avoid Bryce entirely. A telephone call to him this evening would provide the charity information she required. There was no need at all to meet him

again, face to face. The tension began to drain away,
and she strolled around the tent, idly inspecting rows of
graded tomatoes and neat bundles of celery.

The tarpaulin flap swung aside, and a large frame,
quivering with suppressed emotion, loomed beside her.
Caitlin caught her breath as Bryce encircled her wrist in
a vicelike grip.

'Don't try and escape from me,' he growled, pulling
her with him out into the sunshine. Caitlin tottered
along on her high heels as he marched her through the
crush of people. As before they were attracting
interested glances.

'Let me go!' she muttered through her teeth as she
twisted her arm in a vain attempt discreetly to release
herself.

'Fight, and I shall kiss you, here and now. I'm sure
everyone will be delighted,' he threatened. The
harshness in his voice told her he wasn't joking.

Anxiously Caitlin's eyes streaked over the villagers.
She refused to allow herself to be flung into a
compromising situation in full view of everyone, and
Bryce knew it. There was no choice, but to obey. With
rising frustration Caitlin permitted herself to be led
towards the walled garden at the side of the main
house. Their departure was noted with nudges and
winks, she was hotly aware of that. He steered her
through a wooden gate and between tidy beds of tulips,
primulas and forget-me-nots. The brick walls of the
secluded garden were thick with the light green and red
of Virginia creeper, but Caitlin was too dazed to notice.
When they reached a bench, set in a hedged alcove,
Bryce stopped.

'Sit here,' he snapped, pushing her down.

Desperately she summoned up strength to retaliate,
but her nerve ends pounded with fear as he towered
above her like a dangerous alien, his face contorted
with rage. She was tautly aware of him as Slattery, for

the grim hardness of his expression was reserved by the millionaire detective for his sworn enemies.

'You utter bitch!' he spat. 'I told you everything off the record, but you couldn't resist splashing it around, could you?'

Caitlin squinted up into the sunshine. 'I don't know what you're talking about.'

Angrily he paced before her. 'Don't act the innocent,' he sneered, bayonetting her with burning eyes. 'I was right, you're not to be trusted. You're a bloodsucker, just like all the other journalists. You don't give a toss for me, or my life. The only thing you care about is revealing a wonderful scoop.' His voice cracked with pain, but his eyes shone fiercely, quelling any response. 'How much did they pay you?' he taunted.

'For what?' she bleated with difficulty.

'Stop acting,' he ordered. 'You know damn well what I'm talking about—the headlines in this morning's paper announcing my retirement from *Slattery*.' He stalked before her. 'What a bloody mess! The phone's been constantly ringing since dawn. I've had to try and placate my agent, fend off the press, speak to my lawyers, and work out what on earth I do next.' He swore under his breath. 'I don't know where the hell I'm up to!'

'It wasn't me,' she protested weakly.

He didn't choose to acknowledge her denial.

'My life has been thrown into chaos because some infant reporter can't bear to keep the news to herself for five minutes. You didn't waste much time, did you?' he accused bitterly. 'If you'd agreed to wait for a month or two I'd have given you the exclusive.'

'I didn't leak it.' Her voice was stronger now.

Bryce raked a hand through the thick black hair. He prowled up and down, turning on his heel every few strides to retrace his steps, effectively imprisoning her.

'I thought we'd agreed on a truce, but you had to

strike another blow, didn't you, Caitlin? Well, now it's my turn.'

She eyed him warily. His anger was tangible. If she touched him he would probably bite off her hand, and chew up the rest of her for lunch.

'Do you still have that boy-friend of yours?'

The question took her by surprise. 'Yes, why?' she asked guardedly.

Bryce rocked back on his heels and thrust his hands into his trouser pockets. 'Say goodbye to him, Sunshine. He'll not want you around by the time I've finished with you.' His eyes scraped over the gardens and the marquees beyond the wall. 'One thing is certain, you'll be branded as a loose woman as far as this locality is concerned.'

'I don't understand.'

'You've played havoc with my life, and now I intend to play havoc with yours. I shall ruin your reputation well and truly.'

'But I didn't tell anyone of your wish to leave the series.' Caitlin raised a defiant chin.

'You're the only reporter I've told,' he said flatly. 'It has to be you.'

Frantically she shook her head. 'Honestly, it wasn't.'

'When was a reporter ever honest?' he sneered.

'I am,' she said hotly.

'You,' he informed her, 'are just like all the rest, despite your undeniable appeal.' His dark eyes scanned her face. Indignantly she glared back. Electricity began to build between them, crackling through the air. With a rough gesture Bryce abruptly reached down and put his hands on her upper arms, pulling her up to face him. His mouth fastened on hers, taking her by surprise. The kiss burned with fierce rage.

'I don't know whether to hit you, or . . .' he muttered, thrusting her away.

'You don't hit . . .' Caitlin began.

'Slattery does,' he replied in quietly dangerous tones. 'And as you don't seem to know the difference . . .' The rest of his words were left to her imagination.

With shaking fingers she teased the tumbled cloud of curls into a semblance of order, resolutely avoiding his eyes.

'I must go and check on the progress of the judging,' she said briskly.

'We go together. How am I to convince the local population that we enjoy an intimate relationship, if I don't stick to your side like glue?' His arm shot out and encircled her shoulders like a straight jacket. 'Kiss me.'

She lowered her head. 'No.'

Hard fingers grabbed at her chin, forcing it upwards, then his mouth descended. Caitlin raised her knee to deliver a short sharp blow where it would hurt most, but Bryce gave a bark of laughter, and before she could move into action a firm thigh was thrust between hers. His hands were rigid on her shoulder blades clamping her against him. There was no escape. He was far too strong, and the demands of his mouth were changing her blood to quicksilver. As he forced her lips apart her resistance wavered. She was no longer fighting. Of their own volition her arms slid around his neck. His probing mouth was awakening a pagan desire she could no longer deny, and as Bryce explored the satin confines of her lips she arched against him. He lifted his head.

'Enjoying it, Sunshine?' he asked coldly, wiping his mouth on the back of his hand.

Flame filled her face. So the kiss had been a mockery! 'You're a swine!' she flashed.

'And so are you,' he countered.

She looked him up and down. 'Stop being Slattery,' she demanded, her breasts heaving.

'I'm not.' Lazily he smoothed down the black sideburn at his jaw.

'You are! You swagger when you're Slattery—not

physically, it's a mental swagger. I don't like it.'

'Tough!' The word shot out and hit her between the eyes.

Bryce moved towards her.

'Don't you dare touch me again,' she threatened nervously, stumbling back on her high heels.

The wide shoulders shrugged indifferently. 'As you wish, but if you step out of line, I shall make you pay.'

The threat chilled her with an odd mixture of fear and excitement.

Physical touch was superfluous to his subtle strategy. When they rejoined the fête his dark eyes openly caressed and undressed her, his voice purred his adoration and Caitlin became tautly aware he was successfully convincing everyone that they were lovers.

Bryce was a natural focus of attention, and with him at her side it was impossible to avoid contact with a never-ending stream of villagers, each one grist for his mill. With seeming innocence he slipped references into the conversation advising all and sundry that she'd spent time with him in his room at the King's Head. Caitlin began to bristle with fury at his deception.

'I shall go home,' she threatened under her breath as they moved away from a smiling band of Mothers' Union ladies, each one a victim of Bryce's potent chemistry, and each one wishing she was as favoured as the young woman by his side.

'You won't. Any rebellion and I shall do this.' He slid two hands firmly along the side of her breasts and beneath her arms, pulling her against him. For a long moment he held her close until she felt the throb of his muscles.

'Stop it, Bryce,' she pleaded, wishing she could die and escape the amused glances of a host of onlookers.

'Do you behave, or do I kiss you thoroughly?'

'I behave,' she muttered sullenly.

'Good girl,' he smiled, releasing her and giving her

bottom a pat which convinced everyone who was watching of previous familiarities.

After that episode Caitlin kept her feelings of resentment carefully subdued. At times Bryce appeared to be relaxed and enjoying himself, but then a pinpoint of anger would prick in the depths of his eyes, and she realised he was coldbloodedly reaping his revenge.

Publicly his behaviour was impeccable. Without complaint he signed hundreds of autographs, even when they were having lunch. He chatted amiably with the winners of the different competitions as she started to list their names, he tickled the babies under their chins and made them laugh. It was an expertly executed public relations exercise, Caitlin thought savagely. But despite the affable charm, his eyes had a habit of returning to her, weighing her up and always finding her wanting. She chafed beneath his gaze, and wished the afternoon would end.

'Turn it off, Bryce,' she implored, as they went towards the home-baking tent.

He halted on the grass and viewed her arrogantly, clenching his jaw in crisp appraisal. 'Turn what off?'

'Turn off the Slattery charisma.' The plea came from her heart.

'But if I stop being Slattery, then your safety disappears,' he returned, the corner of his mouth twisting with some emotion Caitlin couldn't identify.

'What do you mean?' Her nose wrinkled.

'You're not a blonde, so Slattery won't make love to you.' His eyes raked her from top to toe. 'But I will.'

Hot and cold needles stabbed along her backbone, and she struggled to deny a fever which started low down and rose like a flood into her brain. She raised her head in challenge, but somehow her glittering gaze became caught up with his, and the crowded field faded from her awareness, the noises of the loudspeaker and the laughing children petered away. They stared at each other, each recognising a need.

A hand clapped Bryce on the back, and he spun round, startled. The spell was shattered. Sir Quentin beamed at the pair of them.

'Sorry to interrupt. Would you care to come up on stage now, Bryce, my good fellow? We'd like you to help with the car raffle and present the other prizes.'

Bryce gave a smile of acquiescence. Caitlin noticed that the mental swagger was functioning smoothly. She creased her brow. Perhaps she should be grateful for the millionaire detective. If Bryce's words were to be believed, it was only when he was wearing his public Slattery face that she was free from danger, but when he reverted to being himself she was vulnerable.

'Would you mind if Caitlin came along too?' he asked his host politely. 'I like to keep her near.' Restraining fingers fastened like a handcuff around her arm.

Sir Quentin winked conspiratorially. 'By all means. This is the young lady from the *Bugle*, isn't it?'

The twinkle in his eyes marked her down as one of Slattery's girls, further proof of his virility. Silently fuming, Caitlin stalked on to the stage, and found an end seat on the back row, fervently hoping her presence would not be noticed. A tiny girl, trim in her Brownie uniform, was on tiptoe, reaching up towards the brim of a large drum filled with folded raffle tickets. Fruitlessly her hand waved above them. Bryce chuckled and hoisted her up so that she was able to reach. The little girl plucked out a ticket and then twisted in his arms to grin her thanks. Another admirer, Caitlin thought waspishly. Bryce squatted down beside the child.

'Can you read it out?'

'The winner of the car is Mrs Elsie Richards,' the girl announced importantly, in a high squeaky voice. There was a burst of applause from the arena, and Mrs

Richards appeared at the side of the stage, clapping her hands together in excitement. Caitlin chewed her lip. If she did not know better she would have imagined Bryce had fixed the raffle to make her situation even more incriminating. It would not go unnoticed that Mrs Richards was Desmond's home help, and Caitlin was Desmond's niece, and Bryce was Caitlin's ... She refused to think further. No such thoughts troubled Mrs Richards for she bounded enthusiastically forward, grinning from ear to ear, Desmond hurrying behind her.

'Oh, thank you, thank you, Mr Cameron,' she declared, smiling up at him with a besotted air.

'I trust you will enjoy many happy miles of motoring.' He nodded in the direction of the car displayed in the distance.

'I shall, I shall,' she assured him, blushing with pleasure as he bent to deposit a kiss on her plump cheek. Firmly clutching the voucher to her bosom, she trotted off down the steps, chattering wildly over her shoulder to Desmond. Bryce threw Caitlin an intense look. Keeping track of me, she thought grimly, as he proceeded to distribute the prizes to a procession of winners. She double-checked the names in her notebook, allowing herself the occasional glare at the broad back and tapering hips while she simmered with silent resentment. When the final name was announced she slammed the book shut and made a dive for the steps. Bryce had had his revenge. Enough was enough. All she wanted to do now was hide away in a dark place and allow her bruised ego to heal.

Crossing her fingers that she could make a quick getaway, she mixed into the swarm of villagers, hoping to reach the safety of the car park before he became aware of her departure. When she caught a glimpse of Mrs Richards' flower-trimmed hat ahead in the mêlée, Caitlin steered determinedly towards it. The widow was clutching Desmond's arm, noisily rejoicing over her good fortune.

'Congratulations,' Caitlin smiled as she joined them.

'Isn't it wonderful!' Mrs Richards babbled. 'Fancy me winning a car from Bryce Cameron! I think he's a charming young man.'

'I'd think that too, if he had provided me with a brand new family saloon, free of charge,' Desmond grinned. 'You'll have to allow me to teach you to drive.'

Mrs Richards nodded happily.

'Do you have to take it away now?' Caitlin asked, glancing towards the raised dais.

Her uncle shook his head. 'We've had a word with the manager of the garage. I've arranged to collect it for Elsie one day next week.'

Mrs Richards giggled and put her arm through Desmond's, hugging him close. 'I'm so excited,' she declared gaily. As she looked beyond Caitlin her flushed face became even pinker. There was no need to turn round. Almost by instinct Caitlin's stomach lurched as a proprietorial hand caressed her shoulder. She felt the fiery warmth of his breath on her neck as Bryce bent his head to speak into her ear. The low voice was carefully modulated, exactly pitched to carry into the alert ears of Mrs Richards and anyone else who cared to listen.

'There you are, my darling,' he crooned. 'I missed you.'

The widow's eyes grew round as florins.

Bryce turned and offered her his hand. 'Congratulations again on winning the car. I'm sure you'll find it to be a reliable model.'

Mrs Richards blushed and twittered, explaining how she fully intended to learn to drive, and how Desmond had offered to teach her. Trapped beneath the firm hand on her shoulder, Caitlin stood silently by trying to ignore the grip which was burning through the fine cotton of her dress. A stray finger reached out idly to caress the bare skin of her arm.

'Thank you for the signed photograph,' Mrs Richards chattered on. 'It was very kind of you to pass it to Caitlin for me.'

Inch by inch the girl was sliding her way from his grasp, but the fingers tightened warningly.

'I'd do anything for Caitlin,' he murmured. 'Wouldn't I, darling?'

'You are good friends?' Mrs Richards enquired, her ears flapping. Caitlin squirmed. The reply would be all over the village first thing in the morning.

'Couldn't be closer,' he smiled. The affirmation dripped with innuendo.

'We hardly know each other, dammit,' she defended in temper. Her words ripped through the pleasantries like a knife through an Old Master. Desmond and his lady friend exchanged shocked glances, and her stomach plunged. In their eyes she had acted with extreme rudeness, when all she had intended to do was refute Bryce's allegations. She was aware that her denial had emerged as a peevish slur in the face of his loving attention, and cast around in her mind for some other, more appropriate, means of attack. She came up empty-handed.

'Do you think I could be naughty and ask for a second signed photograph?' Mrs Richards asked coyly. 'For my nextdoor neighbour.' She cast a flirtatious glance at Bryce from beneath the brim of her hat, and when he responded in kind Caitlin began to feel sick. He was smiling graciously, smug in the knowledge that he was being worshipped, yet again.

'With pleasure,' he beamed, then cast Caitlin a sharp glance. 'If Cait would be kind enough to spare a few minutes of her time and accompany me to the King's Head, I'll gladly give her a photograph. Then I'll run her back to the cottage.'

She opened her mouth to issue a polite refusal, but already Desmond was thanking Bryce for his generosity, and shaking his hand. Trapped again, she thought rebelliously, as Bryce kissed Mrs Richards' flushed cheek and smiled farewell.

The Maserati was parked out of harm's way in the courtyard at the rear of the manor house.

'Shouldn't you drive Eleanor back to the hotel?' Caitlin asked, confronting him over the roof of the car.

'No need. She and Frank left hours ago.'

In a fit of pique, Caitlin settled herself down beside him.

'No doubt you feel very satisfied with yourself,' she taunted. 'You laid on a beautifully controlled performance today. I'm surprised you didn't charge entertainment tax.'

'Glad it was appreciated.'

'And apart from ruining my reputation, your fan club must have doubled in numbers.'

A sardonic brow lifted. 'Do you wish to become a fully paid-up member?'

Caitlin swore. 'I would never become a fan of such a low-down, conniving bastard!'

'Language, language,' he rebuked softly, turning the ignition. His mouth was crooked with amusement. 'Next thing you'll be telling me is that you have no intention of coming up to my bedroom to collect the photograph.'

'I don't,' she snapped, folding her arms. 'I shall wait in the car.'

'What are you afraid of?' he grinned. 'Surely, if I'm Slattery, as you keep telling me, then you're perfectly safe?'

As he slid the gear-stick into first she eyed him warily, trying to quell the disturbing realisation that the man beside her seemed to possess a split personality. And if he did, how could she cope?

CHAPTER FIVE

'You could always write up the affair in that magazine of yours,' he remarked, thrusting the car into second, his strong wrist swinging the wheel until they were out of the courtyard.

'What affair?'

'The one everyone is convinced we're enjoying.' He arched a disdainful brow. 'It would probably prove to be a bigger scoop than the news you revealed about me quitting *Slattery*.'

'I didn't reveal anything!'

'There's no one else it could be. I've only hinted my plans to one or two very close friends, and there's no reason at all for them to advise the media.'

His denial of her innocence was absolute. There was nothing else to say. They sat in silence as Bryce steered the Maserati into line among the jam of cars on the drive. Chattering villagers were making their way past the stationary vehicles on their way down to the road. As they came alongside the gleaming Maserati, fingers were pointed, elbows twitched and interested eyes peered through the tinted glass. Unsuccessfully, Caitlin tried to ignore the audience. Her seat in the car beside Bryce only seemed to confirm their relationship, and she edged away from him in an attempt to indicate her presence meant nothing, primly folding her hands on her lap.

He cast a sidelong glance from beneath his dark lashes. 'It's too late now,' he taunted. 'They all think we're sleeping together.' He switched off the engine and leant back, stretching his arms with a feline ease that made her heart pound. The gaping procession continued.

'It's like being in a goldfish bowl,' she complained.

'You learn to accept it,' he said wryly, stroking a finger across the back of her wrist. 'That's where Slattery comes in useful. It's easier if you have a character to hide behind.'

'What will you do when Slattery no longer exists?'

He traced the bones of her hand with a long finger. 'When he goes, so do the flashy car, the weekly television exposure, and, I hope, the fuss.'

'Do the blondes disappear, too?'

'Most of the girls only want Slattery, not me.'

Caitlin found that impossible to believe. Bryce was infinitely more appealing without Slattery's deadly con-man charm. The saloon in front of them began to move, and he switched on the ignition, slowly edging the big car forward.

'What's the location for the film you're making?' she queried. Talking helped to keep her mind off the stares of the passing pedestrians.

'Are you asking as a reporter, or from genuine interest?'

'Genuine interest.'

He studied her, then, when he was satisfied with her reply, said: 'The Seychelles.'

'Fantastic!'

He nodded, giving a small smile. 'That other Eden, set in the middle of the Indian Ocean.'

'I believe the islands are magnificent. I wish I was coming.' The last sentence was added spontaneously, without thinking.

'Do you?' He peaked a brow.

'Almost.' It was time for retreat. 'Are you looking for the usual flock of girls?'

'Why, do you want an audition?'

She trickled her fingers through the drift of chestnut curls. 'Wrong colour, and I intend it to stay that way.'

'I suppose we could always make an exception,' his voice was bland.

'I'd stand out like a sore thumb.'

'And how,' he agreed heavily. 'The blondes would softly murmur "yes", while you yelled "no" at the top of your voice.'

She flushed. 'It's not good for you to be pampered,' she justified. Bryce dismissed her statement with a contemptuous twitch of a shoulder.

The nearness of him in the car was beginning to drive her slowly crazy. Every slight movement as he reached to motivate the engine made her want to touch him. She edged further away. Why were sports cars so unreasonably intimate? she wondered. There was only one thing to do, keep talking.

'How did you first become involved in acting?' she asked.

'Through cars.' Bryce reached into the glove compartment and drew out a packet. 'Smoke?'

When she shook her head he extracted a cigarette and lit it from the flame of a heavy gold lighter. He inhaled deeply and wound down his window, casually hooking one arm along the lower frame.

'When I was a teenager I was interested in rally driving. I became pretty efficient, and was asked to handle a car in a television programme filmed in the Highlands. I developed a reputation for fast driving, and landed one or two parts as a bit player.' He exhaled a spiral of smoke. 'I enjoyed the excitement and decided to become an actor. Everything had seemed so easy until then, but when I enrolled in drama school I quickly realised that there was more to acting than accelerating round corners in a dustcloud.'

'But *Slattery* was the breakthrough?' she queried.

'Breakthrough or breakdown,' he said wryly. 'I can't decide which. However, I'd reached the time in my life when I was desperate for financial security, and it's certainly given me that. Even if the worst should come to the worst, and I'm taken to court for breaking my contract, I'll still have some capital. I won't starve.' He flicked the ash out of the window. 'Mind you, I'm going to have to do some pretty tricky footwork, thanks to your premature announcement.'

Caitlin clenched her teeth.

'I'm damned if I'm going to protest my innocence again,' she told him raggedly.

'Good.'

There was silence. Bryce finished his cigarette and ground it into the ashtray. His eyes began to rake over her. Keep talking, Caitlin thought to herself, keep talking.

'My cousin Joelle is an actress,' she said quickly, to fill the gap.

'Blonde?' he jeered.

She nodded miserably, wishing she'd never spoken. He was adding two and two together, and coming up with the right answer.

'And she wants a role in the *Slattery* film?' he taunted.

'No,' she denied hastily, then, remembering she was in danger of spoiling Joelle's chances, amended it. 'Maybe.'

'It's always the same,' he muttered, his fingers tightening on the wheel until the knuckles were bloodless. Then he shifted sideways to examine her and his expression changed. 'Coax me,' he mocked. 'Perhaps I could wangle a part for your cousin.'

Biting deeply into her lip, she ignored the challenge. 'No.'

He thrust a finger beneath her chin, raising her head until her wide hazel eyes were trapped in his. 'You must have learnt by now that you don't get anything for nothing in this world,' he said quietly.

Caitlin's eyes were drawn to his mouth, to the firm full lips she wanted to taste again. The finger beneath her chin was gently tempting her closer until she was almost ready to sink against him. There was a brisk rapping on her window, and she jumped from him in surprise. It was the village constable.

'Get a move on, sir. You're blocking the drive.'

With startled eyes they discovered that the queue ahead had gone, the way was clear. Bryce chuckled and thrust the car forward. With a loud roar the engine powered down the drive and out on to the road. Ten minutes later they were back at the King's Head.

Bryce uncoiled himself from the Maserati. 'Come on, I'll find you a photograph.'

Caitlin ignored the outstretched hand. 'I'll wait here.'

He shook his head decisively. 'I shall make love to you on the forecourt,' he warned, opening her door and pulling her to her feet in one strong movement. His hands were beneath her armpits and she found herself suspended, her toes barely grazing the ground. With a low laugh he set her down, his hands moving confidently past her breasts, her ribcage, her waist. Three faces were peering from a downstairs window, and Caitlin came to a hasty decision.

'I'll go up with you.'

On winged feet she sped ahead of him into the hotel, past a bright-eyed receptionist, past the barman polishing glasses, past a group of guests. As she reached the staircase she broke into a gallop, desperate to escape the prying eyes. Bryce kept pace, striding beside her, humour threatening to engulf his expression. She waited as he unlocked the door of his room, then darted inside. He threw back his head and laughed.

'Anyone who saw that performance will be convinced you can't wait to get me alone.'

She blithely ignored his amusement, and the racing of her heart. 'Please may I have the photograph? I intend to be out of here in three seconds flat.'

Bryce locked the door from the inside and dropped

the key into his trouser pocket. 'No chance.'

She stared at him in disbelief. 'You can't keep me trapped up here!'

'I can and I will. Your reputation is ruined, but I happen to care about mine,' he pronounced, laughter flickering in his eyes. 'It wouldn't say much for my Slattery sex appeal if you rush back downstairs post-haste.' He pushed aside his sleeve to expose his wristwatch. 'Forty minutes ought to be sufficient.' Tossing his jacket on to the bed, he casually started to unbutton his shirt.

'I'll scream,' she protested, her pulses racing like an overwound clockwork train.

'You won't.' His male self-assurance was inviolate. He knew she wouldn't make a scene and expose herself to further gossip.

'I might.' She opened her mouth and took a deep breath. Hard fingers clamped themselves across her lips, while a second hand loosely held her throat. After a long moment she released her breath in a sigh, and the lower hand moved slowly downwards, across her shoulders, pausing to explore the fine bones. It moved on firmly, across the swell of her breasts, cupping first one and then the other. When she tilted her head the restraining hand covering her mouth fell aside. Now both his hands were moving over her, and Caitlin's knees were weak. The mouth which came down on hers was warm and moist, tenderly coaxing. His breathing quickened with hers, and he held her close against him until the hard length of his body was imprinting itself upon hers.

He tugged at the frilly neckline of her dress and his mouth deserted hers to wander across the smooth line of her jaw to her throat, nibbling and tasting the burning skin.

'Darling,' he murmured huskily as his fingertips moved over her breasts beneath the thin cotton. At his touch her nipples tightened, jutting out in taut desire as she surrendered herself, lost in a world of exquisite sensations. He bent his head and gently mouthed her shoulder, his tongue circling hot patterns on her skin. Caitlin moaned. His hands were roaming her body with increasing urgency. I want to be naked, she thought blindly. I want to feel his hands on the nakedness of my breasts. She almost swooned with delight when she felt the tug of his fingers at the buttons of her dress and he deftly pushed it aside. As his hands closed possessively around the warm globes he trembled, then he began expertly rousing her to a heated pitch of desire she had never known before. Impatiently she fumbled at his shirt.

'Let me,' he groaned, ripping it from him as his hands returned to caress her with feverish desperation.

'I want you, Cait. I want you, I want you.' The words were a melody of love. Deliriously she ran her hands over his chest, absorbing the roughness of the hair, the firm clench of his muscles. Arrows of desire darted along her quivering body as Bryce relentlessly stroked the wine-dark pinnacles of her breasts until she was breathless in his arms, aware only of the ecstasy he was creating.

His hand slid into the silken tumble of her hair. Instinctively she thrust back her head, exposing the beauty of her naked throat and shoulders. His open mouth slurred erotically downwards. He moaned as he buried his head in the fragrant valley of her breasts, then his lips surrounded her nipple, gently pulling and teasing until the flesh was tight and swollen with yearning. She swayed against him.

'I wasn't pretending this afternoon,' he muttered. 'I do want you, even if you did betray me.'

She tensed at his words, struggling to understand their significance.

What made Marge burn the toast and miss her favorite soap opera?

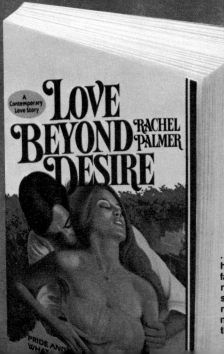

A Contemporary Love Story

LOVE BEYOND DESIRE

RACHEL PALMER

...At his touch, her body felt a familiar wild stirring, but she struggled to resist it. This is not love, she thought bitterly.

PRIDE AND
WHA

A compelling love story of mystery and intrigue... conflicts and jealousies... and a forbidden love that threatens to shatter the lives of all involved with the aristocratic Lopez family.

⌐ Mail this card today for your FREE gifts.

TAKE THIS BOOK AND TOTE BAG FREE!

Mail to: **SUPERROMANCE**
2504 W. Southern Avenue, Tempe, Arizona 85282

YES, please send me FREE and without any obligation, my SUPERROMANCE novel, *Love Beyond Desire*. If you do not hear from me after I have examined my FREE book, please send me the 4 new SUPERROMANCE books every month as soon as they come off the press. I understand that I will be billed only $2.50 per book (total $10.00). There are no shipping and handling or any other hidden charges. There is no minimum number of books that I have to purchase. In fact, I may cancel this arrangement at any time. *Love Beyond Desire* and the tote bag are mine to keep as FREE gifts even if I do not buy any additional books.

134-CIS-KAE4

Name	(Please Print)

Address	Apt. No.

City

State	Zip

Signature   (If under 18, parent or guardian must sign.)

This offer is limited to one order per household and not valid to present subscribers. We reserve the right to exercise discretion in granting membership. If price changes are necessary you will be notified. Offer expires December 31, 1983.

PRINTED IN U.S.A.

SUPERROMANCE ™

**EXTRA BONUS
MAIL YOUR ORDER
TODAY AND GET A
FREE TOTE BAG
FROM SUPERROMANCE.**

↳ Mail this card today for your FREE gifts.

'It doesn't matter,' he said blindly, his mouth returning to hers.

'Bryce, please,' she began, torn between the need for fulfilment and the need to convince him of her innocence. Her honesty *did* matter, it mattered to her. Restlessly she moved against him, trying to stem the rising passion. He must believe her. It was wrong for them to be locked in each other's arms if he still regarded her as a traitor. She slid her hands over the black sideburns, holding his head from hers. 'Bryce,' she said again, but impatiently he jerked his head, loosening her hold, and his hot demanding mouth silenced her.

'Mr Cameron, Mr Cameron, can you come?' A loud rapping on the door accompanied the urgent shouts of the barman. Bryce took a steadying breath and turned.

'What is it?' His deep voice was controlled. Caitlin reeled from him as though she was drunk. He picked up his shirt and began smoothing down his hair in a seemingly effortless transition from passion to normality which grated on her raw emotions.

'Make yourself respectable,' he said, walking towards the door.

Caitlin scowled at the retreating figure and spun away into the bathroom, fastening her dress and trying to damp down the frustration which surged through her veins like a flash flood. The barman's voice carried to her.

'There's a bloke in the lobby from some newspaper, Mr Cameron. Says he's driven up here from London especially to see you. Says he won't move until you've spared him five minutes.'

'I'll be right down,' Bryce replied easily.

As the footsteps receded Caitlin returned to the bedroom.

Bryce heaved on his jacket. 'This interruption is all your fault,' he informed her icily. Now that he had been reminded of her treachery his desire for her had disappeared completely. 'However, I suppose we managed to fill in the forty minutes quite nicely.'

Quite nicely! The pain in her heart trapped her breath. So he had been amusing himself while she, silly fool, had been lost in his lovemaking. She tossed her head, making a vain attempt to rescue her pride. 'I've often wondered how it felt to be seduced by a millionaire detective,' she jeered. 'Now I know. Thank you very much, Mr Slattery.'

She caught the key which streaked across the room and hurriedly unlocked the door. He handed her a signed photograph. For a brief moment their eyes clashed in open hostility, then Caitlin was out of the room and away down the staircase.

Since meeting Bryce in the valley she had kept determinedly clear of Sir Quentin's land, restricting her dog-walking to the road. Although she would have preferred the freedom of the fields, Duke was not concerned. He plodded along happily beside her on the lead, stopping every few minutes to investigate a variety of smells beneath the hedgerow. The road walks would not last for long. Once the television crew departed, Duke would be allowed back on his usual beat, but this time with her uncle in control. Despondently Caitlin kicked at a loose stone, and decided the sooner she was back in London with Matthew, the better. Edgily aware of Bryce in such close proximity in the village, she was tormented by memories of their lovemaking the previous day. Every time a car swept by she stiffened, fearing it would be the powerful Maserati, but it never was, and perversely she experienced a plunging swoop of disappointment.

As she rounded the final bend before the cottage, she was surprised to see cars parked on one side of the lane. A cluster of people were peering over the stone wall, and several children had been hoisted up to sit astride.

The village constable nodded his recognition as she approached.

'Thought you'd be down there with 'em, miss.'

Caitlin joined him.

'Nothing's on the go yet, the action starts around ten-thirty,' he informed her with a smile.

In the distance was the water meadow, now denuded of sheep. Two platforms had been erected to accommodate cameramen and their equipment, one at the edge of the trees, the other on the bank of the river. There was much to-ing and fro-ing between scattered groups of technicians beside the stone bridge as the run-up to filming progressed. The blue Maserati gleamed among a row of vehicles parked in the sunshine. Astonishment yanked up her head and she narrowed her eyes in disbelief. An old Ford, which looked suspiciously familiar, was being driven through the long grass. Caitlin whirled round, giving the lead a swift tug.

'Come on, Duke,' she ordered, and began running towards the cottage, the old dog panting beside her. Her uncle was coming downstairs as she charged breathlessly through the front door.

'Why is your car down by the river?' she demanded.

'It's going to be used in the car chase,' he said placidly as he walked through to the kitchen. 'How many pieces of toast do you want?'

Caitlin was at his back. 'But you love the car, it's an old friend.'

'Too old.'

'You'll be without transport,' she warned.

Desmond searched in the drawer of the dresser for the bread knife. 'That's true.'

'It will take years to save enough money to buy a new car,' she cried unhappily. 'You said so yourself.'

Her uncle shrugged. 'You never know what might turn up.'

Caitlin folded her arms, her eyes suddenly sharp.

'Who did you deal with on the *Slattery* crew?'

'Bryce. I spoke to him yesterday evening when you were out with Duke. Apparently he'd noticed the car when he dropped you off the other day.' Desmond cut four slices of bread. 'He said it would be ideal for their purpose.'

Caitlin swore under her breath. 'How much did he give you for it?'

'Fifty pounds.'

'Only fifty!' She grasped the edge of the table with both hands and leaned furiously towards him. 'It must be worth far more than that.'

Her uncle shook his head. 'I doubt the scrap value would amount to fifty. The car would never have passed the next M.O.T. test. I'd probably have had to pay someone to take it away.' His eyes were trained on the bread beneath the grill. 'In any case the money isn't important. I'm adding it to the cash raised for charity at the fête.'

She released her grip and stared at him with incredulous eyes.

'You mean to tell me that you calmly gave away the car for free?'

'Bryce was very grateful.'

'I bet he was!' Her mind whirled. The television company could easily afford to pay for the ancient Ford, but instead her uncle had been duped, persuaded to part with it for nothing. Bryce had traded on Desmond's naïve generosity, thoughtlessly ignoring the consequences. Now the old man was virtually marooned in his cottage, not strong enough yet to walk into the village, and not wealthy enough to buy another car. Anger blazed in the hazel eyes. Bryce Cameron took first prize for lack of consideration! Another thought leapt into her head.

'You were supposed to collect Joelle from the village this lunchtime.'

'Oh dear, it quite slipped my mind.' Distractedly Desmond shovelled the hot toast on to a plate. 'What shall I do?'

'I'll go down and meet her,' Caitlin offered with a sigh. 'We should be able to carry her luggage between us.'

'She won't be very pleased at the prospect of a two-mile walk,' Desmond grinned ruefully.

'Perhaps we can thumb a lift.'

He gave a nod of satisfaction. 'Yes, two pretty girls like you shouldn't have much difficulty.' His face brightened and he turned to her. 'You could always call in at the King's Head and ask Bryce to bring you home.'

Caitlin grunted. She would rather walk over hot coals than ask Bryce for a favour.

After breakfast she tugged on her anorak. 'Do you want to come and watch the car chase being filmed? It should be exciting. You get a ringside view just along the lane.'

Her uncle picked up the Sunday paper. 'No, thanks,' he said, settling himself down on the sofa. 'I don't feel I could bear to watch the old Ford's last moments. I'll stay indoors and read.'

'The policeman said the action was due to start mid-morning, so afterwards I'll go straight on down to the village and meet Joelle.'

As she retraced her steps there was a loud cheer from the crowd stationed along the wall. Numbers had grown. Now cars were parked nose to tail and the lane was thick with families hurrying along to find a good viewpoint.

'No one's allowed over the wall,' the policeman cautioned as a small boy jumped down on to the grass and then climbed hastily back. 'It's private land, you're trespassing.'

Caitlin found a gap and craned forward. The cars

had been removed and the meadow was almost deserted. She squinted as a bright flash from the lens of a camera catching the sun momentarily blinded her. In addition to the fixed equipment high up on the platforms, other men with handheld cameras were taking up positions on either side of the bridge. The low stone arch had disintegrated and fallen into the river years ago, the smooth, water-rounded boulders still visible in the shallows below.

To Caitlin, the strategy of the chase was obvious. Somehow or other the old car was to be destroyed by falling through the gap between the two slopes of the bridge. She chewed at her lip. If only she could save the Ford before it was too late. Surely an alternative vehicle could be found, one which wasn't the only means of transport for an old man.

The decision was taken from her. There was a gasp from the crowds as two cars shot out of the trees, engines revving, and out on to the meadow. Her eyes widened. She had never seen the Ford, which came second, move so fast in its entire career. With a great roar of horsepower the two vehicles skimmed alarmingly towards the bridge at top speed. The spectators gasped again as the blue Maserati suddenly appeared, racing across the grass in hot pursuit. The first car, a huge white Mercedes, churned along the river bank to leap across the gap in the bridge with only inches to spare. The Ford was not so lucky. Caitlin didn't think it would be. Its speed up the incline of the bridge was too slow. For a second it hovered on the brink of the gap, outlined against the sky, then, as the Maserati closed in behind, the old car sank slowly down to the stones below. There was an excruciating groan of ancient metal. Caitlin cringed. The Maserati soared across the broken arch like a bird, landed in a breathtaking skid, and with a squeal of tyres swung away after the Mercedes. As the cameras followed the continuing

chase a heavily padded stunt man climbed from the
spreadeagled Ford and waded through the water to the
river bank. He ran quickly into the trees as the other
two cars again approached the bridge. After some high-
speed driving the Mercedes also faltered in its flight and
ignominiously joined the Ford on the river bed, while
the Maserati triumphantly powered above them both
and sped away into the valley.

Spontaneous applause burst from the crowds. It had
been an exciting spectacle. Caitlin stuck her thumbs
into the waistband of her jeans and scowled. You are a
very clever man, Mr Cameron, she decided, very clever,
but you won't get away with it. She turned on her heel
and began to march down the lane towards the village.

Pre-prandial drinkers were already gathered along
the bar at the King's Head, but she ignored them all as
she approached the reception desk.

'Is Mr Cameron in?' she asked tightly.

The girl behind the counter grinned. 'You're in luck.
He came back from filming only minutes ago. You're
his girl-friend, aren't you?' Her eyes misted over. 'I wish
I was.'

Caitlin made a noncommittal grunt and moved
towards the stairs. Tongues would be wagging again,
she thought wearily, as the hum of conversation stilled
momentarily behind her. But it didn't matter any more.
Soon she would be back in the comfortable obscurity of
London and village gossip would be unimportant. It
would be a relief to return to Matthew's secure love, for
despite Bryce's threat, it was unlikely he would ever
hear of the so-called affair, and if he did she could
easily explain it away.

Her knuckles were tense as she rapped on the door of
room number seven.

'Come in.'

Once again Bryce was in the middle of his exercise
programme, pressing himself up and down on the

carpet, the taut muscles moving as easily as oiled pistons. He was in jeans and a tee-shirt. Firmly she closed the door behind her, ignoring the astonishment which stretched wide his eyes. The rhythm of his body never faltered. He looked so complacently in control that Caitlin was filled with an urgent desire to shatter that complacency. She walked across and stood before him. Deliberately she stretched out a foot and pressed the ball of her white sports shoe firmly down on the tanned fingers which were spread tautly on the carpet. Bryce gave a furious bellow as the shoe trapped him. With all her weight she pushed down as hard as she could. There was a mixture of oaths and grimaces of pain as he collapsed on to the carpet, then his other hand shot out to fasten, limpet like, on to the back of her knee. Steel fingers jabbed wildly into the soft joint. She tensed her leg, but he was forcing her off balance. Her stance wavered. The pain from his fingers made her clench her teeth. He was compelling her to buckle at the knee. There was no way out, though she tried to pull away and loosen his grip. He was far too powerful. With an undignified thud she sat down before him on to her backside, arms outstretched stiffly, palms flat on the ground. In reflex her foot lifted and his fingers were released.

'Damn!' he swore. 'You could have broken some bones!' He lifted up the large hand and looked at it in consternation.

'I wish I had!'

'Why?' He stretched his pain-numbed fingers gingerly and frowned, then thrust them beneath his armpit and rocked backwards and forwards, comforting himself.

'Because you swindled Uncle Desmond out of his car,' she accused bitterly.

He shook his head. 'I didn't, Sunshine. Your uncle telephoned to ask if the Ford was of any interest for the car chase. I had a word with Frank and he snapped it up.'

Her indignation faltered. 'But Uncle Desmond loved that old car,' she justified. 'Why would he want to get rid of it? He won't have transport now, and he's not well enough to walk down to the village.' Hurriedly she mustered more ammunition. 'And there's no bus route past his cottage.'

The rocking motion ceased as Bryce withdrew his hand and eased his fingers carefully apart. 'He sounded pretty keen to offload it yesterday. He wanted to give it us free of charge, but I persuaded him to take some cash.' Tenderly he felt all over the injured hand with his good one. 'I believe he's given that to charity.' Bryce stuck one of the sore fingers into his mouth and sucked noisily.

'You must have charmed him into it,' she declared. 'Against his wishes. He couldn't have known what he was doing.'

He gave a disbelieving grunt. 'Be reasonable, Cait. I admit to some success with women, but I hardly imagine I have a lethal effect on elderly gentlemen.'

Caitlin put her arms around her upraised knees and rested her chin, surveying him thoughtfully. Perhaps he wasn't the villain she had imagined. Bryce sat before her still sucking away his pain as he waited to shoot down her next attack. Slowly he pulled the glistening finger from his mouth and reached across, rubbing it wetly against her full lower lip.

'Suck it,' he said, pushing the tip a little way into her mouth. 'It still hurts and it's all your fault. Make me better.'

He wore the sulky look of a hurt child, but the glitter in the ebony eyes told her he was all man, with a man's desires and needs.

'Please,' he coaxed.

Caitlin struggled to master the flicker of excitement within her. The long finger slid further between her lips, moving from side to side, slowly seducing away her anger. She opened her teeth and bit it softly. Bryce began to shift across the carpet until he was only a breath away. The intruding antenna probed the smooth inner flesh, then traced the hard line of her teeth. Caitlin closed her eyes, surrendering to his sensual game. When she opened them it was to find Bryce studying her with a disturbing intensity which rocked at her senses. She slithered her tongue along the warm skin and on to the flatness of his nail. Her mouth was full of the taste of him, an infinitely male musky taste which was beginning to intoxicate her. The fever mounted inside her. When she flicked her tongue around his knuckle he made a soft sound of pleasure deep in his throat. Leisurely she drew back her head, releasing him.

'I want to make love to you,' he said quietly, reaching out to mesh his hand in the tangle of silky curls at her neck. His fingers spread, capturing the back of her head, pulling her close. In the moment before his lips met hers Caitlin dimly heard the noisy chorus of car horns outside in the street. It sounded like an argument between drivers. Blearily her mind began to focus into a chain of awareness—cars, buses, Joelle! She had forgotten all about their rendezvous. The bus must have been and gone ages ago. She pushed Bryce away.

'I'm sorry,' she babbled. 'I must go.'

'What's the rush?'

He frowned as she jumped to her feet and began hastily tugging at her hair, then he stood up to face her, his chest rising and falling as he sought control.

'I promised to meet my cousin. She's arriving from London on the bus.' She consulted her watch. 'I've kept her waiting nearly half an hour already, and she'll be furious.'

Bryce rubbed a hand across his brow, and Caitlin glimpsed the frustration which was tightly coiling his muscles.

'Why isn't your uncle meeting her?' he asked, then he answered his own question. 'No car.' He picked up a black leather jacket from the bed. 'I'll come with you in the Maserati and run you both up to the cottage.' He put on the jacket and pulled up the zipper. 'Sorry I'm hot and sticky, but I was unwinding before you arrived. The tension builds up inside when I'm doing the stunts. I can only release it by exercise.' He slipped an arm around her waist, pulling her close. 'Come tomorrow, Cait, and trample me into the ground again. I like the way you make me feel better.' He opened his eyes wide, glancing appealingly at her through his lashes. It was the Slattery look again.

Caitlin moved from him and out into the corridor. A little voice inside her head was telling her that if Joelle's arrival had not broken into her thoughts she would have ended up in Bryce's bed. Like the blondes, and she didn't want that! Bryce was strictly a 'love 'em and leave 'em' merchant, and that was not good enough.

'Come and have dinner with me this evening,' he suggested as they went out on to the forecourt of the hotel.

'I can't. It's Joelle's first day here. It would be unkind to desert her.' It was a lie. Joelle wouldn't care. If their positions were reversed, her cousin would be off without a backward glance.

'Bring her along, too,' Bryce said reluctantly.

'Sorry, but we can't leave Uncle Desmond alone.'

He gave a heavy sigh. 'He can come as well, and the damn dog if necessary.'

Caitlin flashed him a look as they neared the car. Her instinct told her it was dangerous to see him again. Somehow she was sure if they were alone together, just once more, they would wind up as lovers and that, as far as she was concerned, was a one-way ticket to nowhere. Even with her uncle and cousin as escorts she would not feel safe. Bryce had already shown a breathtaking skill at getting what he wanted.

'Thanks for the package deal,' she smiled as he drove the Maserati out onto the road, 'but it's better if I take a raincheck.'

'The fatal charisma doesn't work with brunettes, it seems,' he said lightly. 'Are you sure you don't want to invest in a bottle of bleach?'

'No, thanks, I prefer to be able to resist you.'

'Why?' It was a loaded question. She was searingly aware of the dark eyes scrutinising her profile.

'There's no future in it, Bryce,' she said as flippantly as she could. 'Our relationship has been a series of disasters from start to finish.'

'But it's not finished yet,' he pointed out calmly.

Fever raced crazily through her pulses.

His voice was quiet. 'You don't trust me, do you?'

She rounded on him in astonishment. 'It's you who don't trust *me*! You blame me for leaking that story.'

CHAPTER SIX

BRYCE blithely ignored her outburst, leaving her to smoulder beside him in righteous indignation. When they turned into the bus station a frowning blonde, arms folded, was leaning against a lamp-post, surrounded by a heap of luggage. The pointed toe of a black suede boot clicked irritably on the paving stones.

Caitlin pointed a finger. 'That's Joelle.'

As the Maserati approached, a subtle change took place. The girl straightened, pulling down the blouson top of a clinging scarlet suede suit and smoothing the tight skirt closer around her hips. Her expression cleared. By the time the car braked beside her and Caitlin climbed out, the last remnants of her vexation had been replaced by delighted curiosity.

'Sorry I'm late,' Caitlin apologised with a smile, but already her cousin's interest was elsewhere. Bryce was striding around the car, making Joelle's baby blue eyes open wide beneath their frosted lids. Automatically her hand went to fluff out her halo of pale hair.

'Hello,' she murmured, sliding her other hand along her hipbone, emphasising the curve. Taking a deep breath, she arched her slender body towards him. Caitlin almost laughed out loud at the blatant comehither routine, but as she glanced at Bryce to share her amusement, the laughter froze in her throat. He was smiling down at Joelle, shrewdly assessing her figure and liking what he saw. Caitlin grew cold all over.

'It's my fault Cait wasn't here on time to meet you,' he said, rapidly stacking the suitcases into the boot of the car. 'Please forgive me.'

Joelle viewed the easy movements of his lithe body

with outright admiration. 'Don't worry.' She laid a
manicured hand on the sleeve of his leather jacket. 'I
was perfectly happy waiting in the sunshine.'

Caitlin bit back a protest. Her stomach began to
churn as she watched Joelle and Bryce smile at each
other. The Slattery swagger was switched on to
overdrive, and she turned away with a frown, pushing
her hands into her anorak pockets and tightening her
fists.

Bryce slammed down the lid of the boot. 'Shall we
go?'

'Would you mind sitting in the back, Cait?' Joelle
flashed a bright pleading smile. 'I don't think I can
squeeze through in this skirt.' She trickled her fingers
over a sleek thigh. Caitlin gave a look of exasperation
and climbed into the rear seat without a word. Joelle
slid beside Bryce, carefully arranging her skirt to reveal
long nylon-covered legs.

'I adore your programmes,' she breathed as they
swung out on to the High Street.

'I'm surprised a pretty girl like you has time for
television,' he remarked pleasantly. 'Surely you're too
busy dining and dancing to spend time at home
watching the box.'

'Caitlin and I are *Slattery* addicts,' Joelle assured
him.

'Cait likes *Slattery*, too?' It was more an exclamation
than a question, and the eyes which trapped hers in the
rear-view mirror seemed to be piercing her soul, making
her shrivel inside.

'It was Caitlin who first introduced me to the
programme,' Joelle prattled on candidly. 'She's mad
about it. She refused to go out on Tuesday evenings in
case she missed a single episode.'

A low rumble of laughter came from deep within
Bryce. Caitlin resisted the urge to reach forward and
silently throttle her cousin.

'I'm an actress,' Joelle announced out of nowhere, patting at the blonde halo.

'I never would have guessed.' Bryce was dead-pan.

Joelle pulled down the sunscreen and examined her face in the mirror. 'Do you think I'd be good enough to be a Slattery girl?'

'You'd make a delightful accessory,' he assured her, lifting a brow. 'Come down to the King's Head tomorrow and speak to Frank Stern, the director. Tell him I sent you.'

The sunscreen was pushed aside and Joelle produced one of her dazzling smiles. 'You really mean that?'

'I can't offer you a part, casting doesn't come under my jurisdiction, but I could have a word in the right ear.' His voice was rich with promise, making Caitlin squirm.

Joelle laid her hand on his denim-covered knee. 'I'd be very, very grateful.'

'I'll remember that.' He sounded as though he meant it.

Caitlin stared out of the window. It was eminently possible Joelle would end up in his arms like all the other Slattery girls. Pain tightened across her chest like a steel hawser. She didn't think she could face the prospect of her cousin and Bryce together.

'I'd do anything to be a Slattery girl,' Joelle cooed, and Caitlin tried not to notice as her fingers tightened on Bryce's leg.

'How about coming to dinner this evening?' he asked. Then added, 'With Cait, of course.' Her name sounded like an afterthought and she winced.

'We can't leave Uncle Desmond alone,' she inserted quickly from the back seat. Bryce was doing this on purpose, damn him. They both knew Joelle would never pass up such an opportunity.

'Daddy'll be fine,' her cousin muttered back. She

turned to Bryce, fluttering her lashes. 'He prefers to go to bed early.'

Bryce shot a look of triumph through the mirror. 'Fine. I'll collect you both at eight.'

Resting her chin on her hand, Caitlin stared balefully at the scrubbed face in the dressing table mirror. The decision had been made. She would not be joining Bryce and her cousin for dinner at the King's Head. It was just as well, she thought drily, for Joelle had been hogging the bathroom for the past hour and still there was no sign of an end to her occupancy. Caitlin sighed. She had decided to conjure up the 'flu. It was as good an excuse as any. Only her cousin needed to be fooled and that would be simple. Playing third party to Joelle's outrageous flirting and Bryce's smiling acceptance was totally out of the question. The episode in the car had warned her what to expect. She had no doubt that the evening would develop into an enthusiastic duologue on the glories of the acting profession, interspersed with fruity gossip. Joelle was not a girl to sit on the sidelines and listen, she demanded centre stage. Well, she could be the star of this particular performance as far as Caitlin was concerned. And as for Bryce ... His reputation would be enhanced even further if he dined with *two* attractive young women. She tightened the sash of her dressing gown savagely. She refused to give him that satisfaction.

At a quarter to eight the bathroom door swung open, and Joelle emerged on a cloud of talc and hair lacquer.

'How do I look?' she asked, pirouetting before Caitlin, arms outstretched.

'Gorgeous.'

It was true. Her figure had been poured into silver-metallic pants and a tight white-and-silver-dotted top. High shiny sandals gave her legs the appearance of stretching as far as her shoulders, and her blonde hair had been painstakingly backcombed around her head into a vast dandelion clock. She spun delightedly, then noticed Caitlin's untidy curls.

'Hurry up, you've not much time.'

Caitlin walked over and lay down on the bed. 'I'm not coming. I think I have the 'flu.' She gave what she hoped was a pathetic smile, but the effort went unnoticed for already Joelle was veering towards the door.

'Poor you. I'll make your apologies to Bryce.'

'Thanks,' Caitlin said to sweet nothing. Joelle was slowly negotiating the staircase to an accompaniment of grunts and sighs. The elasticated pants, high heels and steep dark stairs were a dangerous combination, and she was obviously having difficulty. Caitlin grabbed the pillow, turned on to her stomach and thrust it over her head in chagrin. It was illogical to expect a stronger protest. She should have realised Joelle would be delighted to have Bryce all to herself.

When the muffled roar of an engine penetrated the pillow she wrapped the ends closer around her ears, trying to block out all awareness. Miserably she lay there, waiting for the noise of departure, but instead there came a sound on the stairs, hurried footsteps as though someone was bounding up them, two at a time. She only had a split second in which to twist round on to the pillow and adopt a modicum of composure before the door burst open and Bryce was framed on the threshold. He seemed larger than ever in the cottage, his broad shoulders almost spanning the doorway. He was wearing a black suit and snowy shirt. Dressed for a funeral—*her* funeral, Caitlin decided. She looked at him aghast, her temples throbbing with sudden tension.

'What's wrong, Cait?' he asked, raking his fingers through the hair which grew thickly at the nape of his neck. He stepped forward.

'Don't come close,' she warned. 'I think I have the 'flu.'

'You were fine this morning.' It was almost an accusation. Her spine pricked with apprehension as the shrewd dark eyes surveyed her.

'It only came on an hour or so ago.' She pulled a handkerchief from her dressing gown pocket and started to blow her nose. 'Keep away. You might catch my germs and then the filming would be disrupted.'

'Don't talk rot.' He ignored her warning and sat down on the edge of the bed. 'If you do have any germs I'll have caught them already, won't I?' he teased.

Caitlin lowered her lashes in confusion.

'Your uncle won't be alone this evening,' he said gently, reaching for her hand. 'Mrs Richards arrived at the same time as me. They're sitting together watching television.'

He lifted his head and listened. There was the sound of a laboured ascent on the stairs. Joelle wiggled into the room.

'Poor Cait,' she said, making for the bed. 'You don't look well at all.'

'She seems fine to me,' Bryce inserted drily.

Joelle laid a scented hand on Caitlin's brow.

'I'm sure you have a temperature,' she declared.

It was probable. The nearness of Bryce on the bed was creating a tropical fever in her body which Caitlin knew would send the mercury soaring.

'You need a hot drink and a good night's rest,' he said, taking control. 'Which do you prefer—coffee, tea, hot chocolate?'

'Chocolate,' she said meekly.

Bryce turned to Joelle. 'Would you organise that straight away, please.' For a long moment she stared at him, her mouth agape, then she turned and left the room. They could hear her huffing and puffing on the staircase.

'I bet she's never acted as a waitress in her life.' Bryce arched a scornful brow.

Caitlin grinned. It was as though they were two conspirators.

'Take off your robe and get into bed before you catch cold.' He sounded like the family doctor. 'Hurry up,' he said briskly as she hesitated. 'You don't want mouth-to-mouth resuscitation, do you?'

Primly she removed her dressing gown and pulled back the covers. Her white broderie anglaise nightdress was perfectly respectable, with its high frilled neck and long sleeves, but the look in his eyes as she revealed it for a moment before she snuggled down between the sheets made her feel as though she was naked before him.

The stairs creaked again as Joelle began her unsteady climb, and a grin twitched at the corner of Bryce's mouth as they listened to her progress. At last she arrived in the doorway.

'There,' she announced with a satisfied smile and placed a steaming mug on the bedside table.

'Feed a cold, that's the old adage, isn't it?' Bryce pondered. 'You should have something to eat, Cait. What do you fancy? Scrambled eggs on toast, soup, or perhaps a plate of sandwiches?' His expression was straight-faced, but as amusement got the better of him he turned to Caitlin and winked.

'How about some fish, or an omelette? We must build you up.'

Joelle's face paled visibly as he continued his menu. Caitlin joined in the fun, taking ages to debate the alternatives he had suggested, while her cousin waited tensely in the background. When the offer of food was finally refused Joelle's sigh of relief was audible. Now that she was off the hook she brightened up.

'Perhaps it's wise not to come this evening,' she said, straightening the bedspread in a last minute display of concern. 'Matthew might be jealous.'

Bryce frowned at Caitlin. 'Matthew? Is that your boy-friend?'

'Nearly her fiancé,' Joelle cut in, standing back to admire her handiwork.

'Indeed!' The black eyes pinned Caitlin to the pillow.

'They've been going out together for simply ages,' her cousin rattled on. 'Matthew thinks they should be married within the next two months before he takes up an appointment in the States.'

A pensive finger followed the path of the scar across his jaw. 'I didn't realise you were on the brink of matrimony.'

Caitlin stared at him in confusion. She could neither accept nor deny Joelle's reading of the situation. Thoughts of Matthew had scarcely entered her head since meeting Bryce again, and she was not much nearer reaching a decision than she had been when she left London. It was tempting to rush back to the haven of Matthew's undemanding love, but . . .

'You ought to be on the stage too, Cait,' he mocked, his eyes scornful. 'It appears I'm not the only one capable of a beautifully controlled performance. You certainly don't act like a woman about to commit herself to one man for life.'

Her mixed emotions found an outlet in sarcasm.

'Perhaps, like you, I have a split personality,' she sneered.

'Perhaps, but I doubt it.' The reply was enigmatic.

Joelle laid her hand on his arm, determined not to be neglected.

'We'd better leave and give Caitlin the chance to rest.'

'Yes,' he agreed tersely, and allowed himself to be led from the room.

As the sound of the Maserati's powerful engine faded into the night, Caitlin sat up in bed and drank down the

chocolate, though it nearly choked her. Irrationally she
felt ashamed of herself. Ashamed that Bryce believed
she had casually allowed him to kiss her and hold her,
when she was poised to become engaged to another
man. The situation was not like that at all. She had
never committed herself to Matthew. Her thoughts
veered. In any case, what right had Bryce to disapprove
of her imagined infidelity when he was a practised
player at the art? She set the empty mug aside and
slumped beneath the covers. Physically he had captured
her. Just the brush of his lips on hers, and resistance
ebbed away. But what was the point in wanting him
physically if her common sense told her a relationship
with Bryce was a dead end? Like Slattery he believed in
short-lived affairs, like Slattery he had never married,
like Slattery he had an endless supply of willing women
at his beck and call. Hadn't Joelle's reaction proved
that?

The two men in her life were diametrically opposed.
At best she could expect a few exciting months with
Bryce, whereas Matthew offered a lifetime of loyalty.
To any level-headed person the choice was obvious.
And yet, and yet . . . As she remembered the caress of
Bryce's mouth on her body the slow burn of excitement
began to infuse her. She lay there, thinking about him.
When she looked at the clock it was still before nine.
How time dragged. Caitlin climbed out of bed and
pulled on her dressing gown. It seemed pointless lying
in bed driving herself crazy.

She was surprised to discover the living room in
darkness when she walked in. Her uncle and Mrs
Richards were sat close together on the sofa, gazing
into the fire. Duke slowly stretched himself and walked
over, rubbing against her legs.

'Switch on the light, love,' her uncle instructed as she
paused to stroke the dog. When the table lamp
illuminated the room he put his arm around Mrs

Richards and squeezed her. They exchanged a shy smile.

'We've something to tell you. Elsie's agreed to be my wife. You're the first to know.'

Caitlin stared at them in surprise for a second, then laughed delightedly.

'That's wonderful! I know you'll be very happy.'

There were hugs and kisses all round.

'I'm going to sell my little terraced house and move in here,' Mrs Richards said when all the commotion had died down. 'Desmond's providing our home.'

'But you're providing the transport!' he broke in with a smile.

'So that's why you didn't mind losing the Ford,' Caitlin exclaimed.

'I was jumping the gun a little,' he confessed, growing pink. 'I had a hunch Elsie might accept me.'

His bride-to-be dug him in the ribs. 'You only proposed so you could get your greedy hands on my lovely new car,' she teased. Everybody laughed.

The cottage was silent the next morning when Caitlin returned from walking the dog. She hung the lead on its hook in the porch and followed Duke into the kitchen.

'Hullo!' she said in surprise, for Joelle was sat, elbows on the table, staring bleakly ahead, the remains of her breakfast scattered around her. 'Where's Uncle Desmond?' Caitlin reached for the bread-bin.

'Up like a lark,' Joelle replied dully, dragging tired fingers through the neglected tousle of silvery hair. 'Gone to see his lady-love.'

'Isn't it great that they're going to be married?'

'Great.' The unfeeling word dropped like a stone.

'What's the matter?'

'That.' A scornful hand was flung in the direction of a buff folder on the edge of the table.

'What is it?'

'A script. Frank Stern gave it to me last night. He's told me to learn the whole of Scene Three if I want to audition for the *Slattery* part.'

'Well?' The director's request sounded reasonable to Caitlin.

'It's pages and pages,' Joelle moaned. 'It'll take ages to learn. Heavens, I only want to be a Slattery girl. You don't need to be a dramatic actress for that!'

'He's probably testing you. If you give a good reading he'll realise you're genuinely keen.'

Joelle scowled at the folder. 'I can't learn that lot.'

'This might be your big chance. If you were seen as a Slattery girl it could lead to bigger and better parts.'

She lifted her coffee cup. 'Do you think so?'

'You can't expect to be famous unless you're dedicated,' Caitlin said. 'Think of Bryce. He attended drama school, then spent years perfecting his art. And in addition to acting he organises the stunts. They are highly sophisticated operations, needing concentration and attention to detail. Also he exercises regularly to be fit and keep his reflexes sharp. He spends hours in preparation before even one inch of film is shot.'

'But it all looks so easy on the television,' Joelle commented.

'Only because there are long hours of hard work behind the scenes.' Caitlin paused. All of a sudden she was seeing Bryce in an entirely new light. Like Joelle she had glibly dismissed the series, and its star, as lightweight, but on consideration she realised she was wrong. The subject, a playboy detective, might be fanciful, but it was impossible to deny the quality of the series. There was nothing amateurish about it. Indeed, it was acted and filmed with finesse by professionals, each episode a finely-honed blend of excitement, comedy and romance. As her mind flashed back she reappraised the Slattery girls. It had never occurred to her that they needed to be good actresses, but on reflection they had all been up-market blondes, like Eleanor. Actresses with style, flair and impeccable timing.

'Bryce is dishy, isn't he?' Joelle mused, resting her trouser-clad legs on the chair opposite beneath the table. Now that she had momentarily abandoned thoughts of the script her expression was cheerier.

'All that masculine energy,' she giggled.

Caitlin bent her head, recognising the jealousy which twisted through her like a knife.

'He's a sexy devil,' her cousin continued dreamily. 'When he touches you, it makes your bones melt, doesn't it?'

Caitlin busied herself buttering toast.

'Did you have a good time?' she asked, trying to keep a degree of normality in her voice.

'Wonderful. It was just like dating Slattery.' Joelle warmed her hands around the coffee cup. 'Wait until the crowd in London hear about my affair with Bryce.'

'Affair?' Caitlin asked weakly.

Joelle whirled a hand vaguely through the air. 'Well, you know.'

Yes, she *did* know. 'What time did you arrive home?' she asked.

Joelle paused before answering. 'Why? Did I wake you?'

Caitlin shook her head. 'No. I slept solidly from ten until eight.'

'I can't be too exact about the timing,' her cousin said, staring down into her cup. 'Around three, I imagine.'

Caitlin closed her eyes, but the scene was vivid. Joelle and Bryce entwined in each other's arms in the darkness of his room.

'I'm returning to London this afternoon,' she announced quickly. 'Now that you're here to keep an eye on your father I might as well leave.'

Joelle examined a chipped nail. 'If that's what you want. Matthew will be delighted. He came round once or twice to ask if I could persuade you to return earlier.'

'I'm looking forward to seeing him again.' The throb of conviction in her voice surprised her. Suddenly she was desperate for the comfort of Matthew's presence. He would never leap into bed with a chance acquaintance.

'How long will you stay on in Derbyshire?' she asked Joelle.

The girl shrugged. 'For a week or two, I guess.'

That meant until Bryce moved on.

Joelle reached over and picked up the script. 'I'll have to be back in London for the audition. Then, if I'm lucky, I'll be flying off to the Seychelles.' She tucked the folder beneath her arm and walked out of the kitchen, humming contentedly.

'Hurry up, Matthew,' Caitlin implored under her breath, willing him to come with every fibre of her body. Never before had she been so eager to see his familiar face. At the sound of footsteps in the outside hallway, she rushed to fling open the door and threw herself into his arms.

'There, there.' He patted her back comfortingly, surprised at the force of her welcome. 'You *are* pleased to be home.'

She clung to him in speechless relief, burying her head in his shoulder.

'When did you arrive?' he asked, carefully disengaging himself from her embrace.

'An hour ago. I rang you immediately.'

Matthew glanced across at the telephone. 'You've left it off the hook.' His tone was mildly critical. He didn't approve of rash actions; telephones were intended to be in working order.

Caitlin nodded. 'I refuse to waste my time advising Joelle's army of admirers that she's not here. I've had three calls already. They'll have to make do with the engaged signal until she returns.'

Deliberately she had pushed aside the idea that Bryce might ring. Doubtless he would be too engrossed with Joelle to spare her a second thought, but if he should decide to telephone, then he would be unlucky. And serve him right! She was not prepared to share his affections with her cousin.

Matthew sat himself down at the end of the sofa. 'Did you have a good time?' he asked, crossing his legs.

'I enjoyed being in the countryside again. Uncle Desmond has almost fully recovered. He's getting married again, so he'll have a wife to look after him.'

Matthew fixed his eyes on her. 'Joelle told me Bryce Cameron was in Derbyshire.'

Caitlin was suddenly wary. Was that a hint of suspicion in his voice?

'That's right,' she said lightly. 'I wrote an article about him.'

He looked down, inspecting his nails. 'Joelle imagined you and he would be getting together.'

She laughed gaily. 'Don't take any notice of Joelle. You know she makes sweeping statements which mean nothing.'

'Did you see much of him?' It was beginning to sound like an interrogation. Her negative reply came a fraction too late, for Matthew turned to confront her. 'You've fallen for him!' he declared. As the colour rose in her cheeks his conviction strengthened. 'I suspected you fancied him when I saw you together at the theatre. You were both totally wrapped up in each other.'

'We were arguing,' Caitlin protested hotly, beginning to recover her poise.

'You were so involved with him, you hardly recognised me,' he accused, then spread his hands magnanimously. 'I don't blame you, he's a good-looking chap.'

She let out a sharp breath of irritation. 'So he's good-looking, so what! That doesn't mean every woman he meets is going to fall at his feet.'

'I bet he had a damn good try at getting you into his bed.'

For a moment she faltered, remembering their mutual desire. Her silence was proof enough for Matthew.

'There!' He was triumphant.

'I only interviewed him,' she said flatly.

'I understand,' he smiled, patting her hand. She snatched it away.

'Don't be so damned patronising. I didn't do anything.'

'You don't need to feel guilty,' he assured her.

'I don't!'

'I realise these things happen.'

'Not to me,' Caitlin shrieked, rising to her feet and glaring down, hands on hips, chest heaving.

Matthew cleared his throat. 'We'll say no more about it, Cait. I forgive you.' He grinned encouragingly. 'Now suppose we fix a date for the wedding?'

The question was ignored. 'Forgive me!' she shouted. 'I don't want your forgiveness.' Her face grew pink. 'It doesn't bother you what happened between Bryce and me, does it? And you felt the same way about my friendships with the other men. Because I'm intelligent and pretty you have pencilled me on to your blueprint for life as the ideal wife. I'm just an ingredient, a part of your success, and you're prepared to overlook any minor discrepancies, so long as I conform in the main.' She stalked towards the door and flung it wide. 'But you've miscalculated. Your second-rate loyalty is no substitute for love. Get out, Matthew. If you really cared you would be furious.'

He walked over and jabbed a finger beneath her nose.

'I've been very kind and very patient,' he told her righteously. 'You'll be sorry when I'm not around any longer. Don't imagine Bryce Cameron will be so understanding. He'll love you and leave you.'

Her fingers tightened around the edge of the door. 'Get this straight, Matthew. Bryce and I are not lovers. Probably we will never ever see each other again.'

He looked dubious. 'Well then,' he said slowly, his face clearing, 'what are you making all the fuss about?'

'Get out!' she screamed. 'It's over.'

He took a last look at her burning eyes and scuttled away.

It was only when the street door slammed shut that Caitlin realised what she had done. Weakly she collapsed against the door frame, but after a moment or so a smile tugged at her lips. Two years of Matthew's doglike devotion had been terminated in minutes. Bryce had unknowingly made the decision for her and, she admitted, he had done her a favour.

It was two weeks before Joelle returned to the apartment. Two weeks during which vivid pictures of her cousin and Bryce together filled Caitlin's brain. Two weeks when she tossed and turned at night, reliving his every touch, the feel of his mouth, the urgency of his hands on her willing body. So willing. If he arrived on her doorstep now she knew she would take him in. How could she resist? Two weeks which proved to her that she loved him. But it was a worthless exercise. Bryce was an actor, and actors were notorious for short-lived relationships. He had already proved his fickleness with Joelle, what further indication did she need of his attitude towards love? She knew she wasn't emotionally equipped to move into his life, and then move out again a few months later. Love to Caitlin meant caring so deeply that you committed yourself to your partner for life. Love was more than passionate hours in bed. It was companionship, and fidelity, and trust. But neither Bryce, nor she, trusted each other, and how could love exist without trust?

She decided she must set about the difficult task of forgetting Bryce. With a vengeance she threw herself into her work. She compiled a lengthy reading list and staggered home from the library with piles of books. Resolutely she ploughed through them, with the idea that they were supposed to enrich her mind, but secretly she voted them a failure. Bryce's image still intruded.

It was a relief when Joelle at last returned.

'All this washing,' she groaned, tipping a mountain of clothes from her suitcase on to the bed.

'How's Uncle Desmond?' Caitlin asked as the mountain was flung in all directions, underwear landing in one corner of the room, brightly-coloured blouses and satin pants in another.

'Fine. He's been running in the new car. He and Elsie want to sell her house before they take the plunge, then it's all systems go.' Joelle surveyed the clothes with disapproval. 'The launderette will have to wait. It's the *Slattery* audition tomorrow.'

Caitlin's pulses kicked over. 'Have you learnt the script?'

Her cousin gave a satisfied grin. 'You should be proud of me, Cait. I spent days and days working on it at the cottage and now I'm word-perfect.'

'Did you see much of Bryce?' The question was out before she could stop herself, and yet she feared the answer. The world slowed to a halt as she waited.

'He was tied up filming, then he went to Scotland,' Joelle pouted. 'He's had a very busy time straightening out his future. I understand he's leaving for the Seychelles any day now.' She drew her plucked brows together and turned to Caitlin. 'What happened between you two?' she demanded.

'Nothing.' Caitlin took a deep breath. 'Why?'

'He was cut up because you left so quickly. He demanded to have your phone number, and then accused me of deliberately giving him a false one because the number was permanently engaged.'

'I left it off the hook.'

Joelle tossed the last nightdress aside, her thoughts already drifting ahead. 'Well, it's fantastic to be back in the city. Derbyshire was deadly boring.'

London was deadly boring too, Caitlin decided uncharitably the next day. The general office was quiet. Everyone had gone to lunch and she alone remained, desolately sorting out her notes on the morning's interview with an up-and-coming disc jockey. She chewed so savagely at her pencil that the wood snapped. With an impatient finger she began picking the slivers from her tongue. The disc jockey had reminded her of Bryce, he had the same confident masculine appeal. He had asked her out to dinner, but she had refused. Much to his surprise, she thought, with a quirk of her mouth. Like Bryce, it would be rare for him to be turned down. But he would be fickle, too. The eagerness Bryce had shown in contacting her had died a sudden death, for there had been no letters, no further phone calls, and he had made no attempt to reach her at the office. Unflattering it may be, but she had to agree she had been a standard case of 'out of sight, out of mind'.

'Are you economising and eating pencils for lunch these days, or are you off on a vegetarian kick?' a voice intruded.

Caitlin fingered away the last snippet of wood and grinned at Alison. 'I'm full already. You should have seen the spread which was laid on for me this morning—shortbread, cream cakes, meringues and lashings of Irish coffee. Quite a mixture—mind you, the interview was as prolific as the food.' She gestured towards the pile of notes on her desk.

'How was our fledgling dee-jay?'

'Talkative.'

Alison nodded. 'Good girl. That sexy smile of yours seems capable of loosening up the most reticent of stars.' She pulled up a chair. 'I've been fixing up a special assignment for you. The editor and I were forward planning and we've decided to run a feature on television detectives. They are the cowboys of today, let's face it, substituting fast cars for horses. When you count up, there is a whole range of British and American actors finding fame as private investigators.'

'Male sex symbols,' Caitlin said cuttingly.

'Correct. We'll have oodles of photographs of hairy-chested guys, all spouting their private hopes and fantasies. It's bound to be a winner.'

She examined the remains of her pencil. 'And?'

'And for starters we want you to use that sexy smile and fly to the Seychelles to interview Bryce Cameron.'

Her heart looped the loop. 'No, thank you,' she replied as evenly as she could.

'That first disastrous interview took place ages ago. You're far too professional now for him to pull any wool over your eyes, Honeybun,' Alison coaxed. 'Besides, the whole thing will work to your advantage. He'll be so eager to make amends he'll probably spill the beans on the new direction his career will take when the film is completed. So far he's been very tight-lipped.'

'I'd rather not,' she pleaded.

Alison dropped the motherly approach and sternly folded her arms. 'I don't like to pull rank, but you're just the girl for the job. You're going.'

It was useless to argue. As Alison had pointed out, she was a professional. Interviewing Bryce was a job of work, her private feelings did not count. Goosepimples

shivered along her spine at the prospect of seeing him
again. How could she muster up sufficient poise to deal
with him calmly and coolly? She was still toying with
the thought that evening when Joelle shot through the
door, laughing uproariously and clutching a bottle of
champagne.

'I made it, I made it!' she yelled, kicking off her shoes
and rushing into the kitchen to locate some glasses.
'Now I'm a Slattery girl!'

Caitlin thrust aside her own thoughts and hugged her
cousin, joining in her delight.

'Did you remember all the words?' she asked with a
grin.

'Naturally.' Joelle threw back an arm. 'Friends,
Romans, countrymen,' she declared. 'Then I wiggled
my bum, that really clinched it.'

'Congratulations! You'll end up as Dame Joelle yet.'

'Five weeks in the Seychelles,' her cousin beamed,
pouring out the champagne. 'Don't you envy me?'

Caitlin shook her head. 'No need, I'm going out there
as well.' She laughed out loud at the sheer astonishment
which greeted her words, and rattled off the story of her
special assignment as Joelle listened with wide eyes.

'Isn't that fantastic?' Joelle spluttered as the bubbles
of the champagne caught in her throat. 'Both of us in
paradise—perhaps we'll be flying out on the same
plane.'

Caitlin was secretly relieved when it was arranged for
her to travel out three weeks later than her cousin. She
had no wish to be propelled into a fraught situation
with Joelle and Bryce. All she wanted to do was keep a
low profile, and she deliberately asked for a booking at
a different hotel from the film company. It would be far
easier to control her fragile emotions if she avoided a
surfeit of Bryce and Joelle. Or Bryce and any other
woman for that matter.

'I'll keep Bryce warm for you,' Joelle giggled over her

shoulder as she struggled down to the waiting taxi, loaded with suitcases.

'Don't bother, he'll be warm enough.' The reply was brisk. 'The Seychelles are only four degrees from the Equator.'

CHAPTER SEVEN

FOR the sixth time in as many hours the overweight woman in the next seat squeezed past on to the gangway, breathlessly apologising for the disturbance. Caitlin smiled back wearily, then, as the woman heaved herself away, pushed the small beige pillow beneath her head and leant back, lashes spread on her pale cheeks. The Boeing 707 from Heathrow was full to capacity and sleep proved to be elusive. In addition to the woman's trips back and forth there was the constant babble of conversation, meals being served, drinks being dispensed. She had tried to rest, but her mind circled relentlessly. The prospect of meeting Bryce became more alarming as each hour passed.

By the time the pilot announced that they would shortly be arriving at the International Airport of the Seychelles, Caitlin was mentally and physically exhausted. It was a relief to discover everyone else appeared to be half dead, too, after the long flight. It was four o'clock in the morning, a low period on the body clock, she consoled herself as automatically she went through the motions of collecting her suitcase and passing through customs.

A looselimbed American with a dark Mexican-style moustache joined her in the queue for taxis and nodded happily. She vaguely recalled seeing him on the plane, and returned his broad smile with a wan imitation of her own. Numbly she wondered how he could feel so aggressively bright at such an unearthly time of the morning. All she wanted to do was crawl into bed.

'Are you staying at Beau Vallon Bay?' he asked, his eyes parading over her pale-blue safari suit in blatant appreciation. When she nodded he suggested they share a taxi, and as Caitlin told the driver the name of her hotel, he chuckled.

'Me too. I hope we'll be able to see more of each other during our visit.'

Too tired to protest, she nodded weakly. Being chatted up in the wee small hours did not appeal to her, but the American's faculties were in full working order, undimmed by the journey, and he chatted on, without pause, throughout the half-hour drive. Caitlin eyed lush clumps of tropical vegetation at the side of the narrow road, and wished he would shut up.

By the time they reached the hotel he had recited his entire life story, from cradle to the present minute. The facts that he was turning twenty-seven, called Chuck by his friends, and came from Flagstaff, Arizona, dimly penetrated.

'Near the Grand Canyon,' he informed her heartily. 'It's like me, big and wide.'

Caitlin returned a weak smile, despite her drooping eyelids. When a dark-skinned Seychellois porter appeared to whisk away her luggage, she was gratefully released from Chuck's company, and staggered to her room, where she fell fast asleep within minutes.

When she awoke the next day, it was afternoon. She took a long refreshing shower, then slipped a white towelling shift over her bikini and walked out on to the balcony. As the balmy air floated over her limbs in a soft caress, she smiled. Her room was on the first floor, overlooking trim lawns surrounding a kidney-shaped pool where holidaymakers swam and splashed in the blue waters. Beyond the pool was a paved sun terrace, then a few steps down to silver-white sands and the shimmering sea beyond. Dusky maidens in batik sarongs circulated among the guests, bringing drinks and snacks to tables in the shade of fan-shaped travellers' palms.

Indolently, Caitlin stretched out her arms and yawned. Never had the air been so crystal clear, the sky so blue, the drifting fronds of trees so green. No pollution, she thought, remembering that the Seychelles archipelago was hundreds of miles from the nearest land mass of East Africa. Smiling contentedly, she collected her suntan lotion, towel and dark glasses, and wandered down to join the other guests on the terrace. Alison had allotted her a week in the sun, and it seemed wise to spend the remainder of the day relaxing and recovering from her jet lag. Her wits must be sharpened to stilettos before she met Bryce. Tomorrow was quite soon enough to discover the location of his hotel, and she would contact Joelle then, too.

After oiling her limbs she stretched out full length on a lounger. Drugging warmth rolled over her and she succumbed to a delicious half slumber.

'Hi, remember me?' Her drowsy solitude was shattered as Chuck squatted down beside her. She opened her eyes lazily.

'Big and wide, like the Grand Canyon,' she replied with a touch of asperity.

He laughed. 'I looked for you at lunch,' he said, his eyes wandering freely over the glistening curves barely concealed by the brown satin bikini.

'I've only just climbed out of bed and I still feel tired.' She lowered her lids pointedly, but Chuck was not so easily deflated.

'Fancy a swim? The water's great.'

'No, thank you.'

'How about a drink? They serve a fantastic rum cocktail.'

She raised herself on her elbows and surveyed him. 'I'd like to rest right now, if you don't mind.' A smile took the sting from her words. He was rather attractive, she decided.

'Have dinner with me at eight.'

It was apparent that the only way to regain her peace was to accept the invitation.

'Thank you, I'd like that.' She sank down again on the lounger, firmly closing her eyes, and heard Chuck move reluctantly away.

After a carefully-timed spell in the direct blaze of the sun, she pushed the lounger beneath the shade of a bending palm and sat up against the back-rest, looking around her. Crescent-shaped Beau Vallon Bay was fringed with leafy takamaka trees. The hotel was towards one tapering end, and she gathered from groups of sunbathers in the distance that there must be one or two other hotels dotted along the beach. Heavily wooded granite peaks formed a protective backdrop, and as she surveyed the scene a gaudily striped parachute floated out above the ocean, a laughing teenager suspended from the harness. Windsurfers with red and yellow sails leisurely rode the waves, and a lone water skier circled in the bay. Caitlin heaved a sigh of delight. A week in the tropical sunshine would be bliss, and with luck she would develop a golden tan to take back to London. Tomorrow, she decided, she would try and fix the interview with Bryce. The sooner their meeting was over, the better, then she would be released from the tension which tightened her features as she thought of him again. Caitlin gave a mental shake of the head and ordered herself not to be so silly.

The afternoon mellowed. A trickle of hotel guests congregated around the open-air bar at one end of the terrace, while others disappeared to their rooms to change for the evening's activities. Caitlin decided to explore. She stepped down on to the warm stone, then jumped into the sand. It trickled softly between her toes like fine white flour. When she dabbed a tentative foot in the clear waters of the Indian Ocean it was like stepping into a warm bath. Tiny multi-coloured fish darted around in the shallows, alarmed at her disturbance.

The sun was beginning to sink in the sky as she made for rocks which were tumbled across the sand at the far end of the bay. Dragging her toes sensually through the small waves, she started walking along the edge of the surf. The azure sky was fading into soft turquoise green. Other holidaymakers, alone or in couples, were wandering along the sand, basking in the tranquil mood of the late afternoon. Occasionally a more athletic visitor would pound by, returning several minutes later in a mad dash along the sand. When she heard the soft pad of a jogger behind her, Caitlin swerved a little deeper into the water to allow him to pass, but the steps slowed behind her. Chuck, she thought, with a flicker of impatience, but a low voice with a familiar Scottish burr said, 'Hullo, Sunshine. I've been waiting for you to show up.'

Her heart stopped dead for a second. Caitlin whirled round. Bryce was standing, hands loosely placed on lean hips, smiling at her, his bottom lip caught provocatively between his teeth. Subconsciously, she noted that he was tanned to the colour of teak and glistening from his run along the shore. He brimmed with good health, and the sight of his powerful frame in the brief swim trunks made Caitlin's chest grow tight. Speechlessly, she stared at him.

'I'm the reason for your journey, remember?' he teased, putting his head on one side and grinning at the surprise in her wide eyes.

Quickly she pulled herself together. He had the satisfied air of a man who knew something she didn't. Warning signals began to flash in her brain.

'I'm here on business,' she said quickly, the adrenalin coursing through her veins at a hundred miles an hour. 'You're just the first in a series of articles.'

'Just?' He drew out the word into a mocking

challenge, turning down the corners of his mouth into a gesture of laughing dismay. Something in his smug male confidence began to rile her.

'I decided to start with the small fry and save the luscious American guys for later,' she informed him tartly, her eyes flashing.

His good humour was immune to her scorn.

'Liar,' he laughed, his teeth startling white against the sultry tan of his face.

Caitlin's mouth tightened a fraction. She turned away to resume her walk along the bay, kicking at the shallows impatiently. Bryce fell in beside her, but she stared ahead, rejecting his amused glances. He interlaced his fingers with hers, and when she tried to disentangle herself he laughed again, and held on tighter.

'I told you once you were gorgeous enough to be a Slattery girl,' he slanted, 'but you're far too good for old Slattery. I want you to be my girl, a Cameron girl.' As he spoke his dark eyes were sweeping over her, mentally photographing every luscious curve for his own private album.

'No, thank you.' Caitlin stemmed the tremor of her traitorous heart. 'I've no time for fraternising.'

'What's wrong with—fraternising, as you so quaintly put it?' he teased.

'I'm here to do a job, that's all,' she said briskly.

'You're here because Alison sent you, and she only sent you because I arranged it,' he told her calmly.

'No!' She gave a yelp of protest, swinging to confront him.

He nodded, the black eyes suddenly serious. 'I gave her a buzz in London before filming started and we came to an agreement.' He winked mischievously. '*You*, in return for the lowdown on my future. World exclusive.'

His merriment infuriated her.

'Big deal!' she snapped, then her brows knitted together. 'But I'm doing a series.'

'Perhaps Alison has changed it into a series,' Bryce shrugged, 'or perhaps she's not been one hundred per cent honest with you, but you are definitely here at my sole request.' He put his hands on her shoulders and pulled her towards him.

'Request!' Caitlin hurled. 'Cast iron order, you mean. You know damn well Alison would never forgo the chance of a scoop like that. It's not fair. The two of you have set me up.'

'Perhaps, but why all the fuss? Here you are, staying in a luxury hotel, on a tropical island, all expenses paid, and it's thanks to me.'

The proprietorial grip of his fingers on her smooth shoulders was intruding into her consciousness. His fingertips were burning into her, branding her as his property, but for how long? With a sudden furious movement she twisted out of his grasp, making Bryce take a step back in surprise.

'And I suppose you'll do your level best to ruin my reputation here, too?' she declared.

He shifted uncomfortably as his good humour fell away. Caitlin was surprised to see embarrassment on his face when he spoke.

'No, I won't,' he said quietly. 'I behaved disgracefully in Derbyshire at the fête. It won't happen again.'

'You'll keep away from me?' she asked, her heart filling with a strange despair.

'No.' It was a plain statement of fact, and although Caitlin examined him warily she was unable to detect any emotion in his dark eyes.

'Aren't you pleased to be here?' he asked, sweeping an arm to encompass the setting sun which was filling the sky with myriad rosy hues.

'It's very nice,' she agreed, following the flourish of

his hand. She was damned if she would fall over herself with gratitude.

'Nice must be the understatement of the year,' he grinned, his confidence returning. 'Surely you've never seen sea so clear, birds so colourful.' As if to prove his point a brightly plumaged fruit pigeon flew from the trees.

'It's beautiful,' she conceded.

'And so are you,' he told her softly, the firm hands returning to hold her, the balls of his thumbs circling sensuously on the tender hollows at the base of her throat. Dusky shadows of the approaching night concealed the look in his eyes. Slowly his fingers slid over the crest of her shoulders and he held her close. Caitlin swallowed deeply, trying to rake up the enthusiasm to protest. But it was no use, his touch was sending darts of pleasure through her burning flesh.

'I wanted you here,' Bryce said, his lips brushing her ear and moving on to her cheek.

A tremor swept through her body. 'Why?' she asked weakly.

The firm hands slid down her shoulder blades to her hips, pulling her hard against his thighs.

'You know why,' he said huskily. 'I can't make it much clearer.'

A laughing group of children appeared out of the trees and ran down the beach into the water. In the moment that Bryce was distracted she took her chance and pushed him away. She heard him sigh in the dusk, but he accepted her rejection and walked beside her as she continued her path along the bay. Tension coiled within her, and she closed her eyes in dismay. Had he any suspicion of the turmoil his words had created? She wanted him too, desperately, but not for only a week, a month. Not for a year, if she was lucky. She escaped into mundane matters.

'Where's your hotel?'

Bryce pointed into the distance. 'Further along the shore. You can see coloured lights in the trees surrounding the barbecue area.'

'How's the film progressing?' Caitlin was growing calmer as she spoke.

'Very well. All the outdoor sequences, car chases, helicopter dashes, that kind of thing, are completed. Everyone is highly satisfied with the footage.' He was matching her businesslike tone.

'How's Joelle?' The question was supposed to be flipped in casually, but Caitlin's voice cracked. She hoped he hadn't noticed.

'Okay, I suppose. Frank was pleased with her performance.'

'Are there many other Slattery girls in the film?'

'Two,' he replied impatiently. 'But I'm afraid I can't provide you with a report on them because, quite frankly, I don't keep track of their movements. They're the usual type.'

Blonde and beautiful, she thought grimly, and beddable.

'Is Eleanor well?' she asked before she could stop herself. It was an association of ideas.

'I haven't seen her since I left Derbyshire,' he said heavily, biting at the words. He put a hand on her arm and drew her to a halt. 'Why don't you come right out with it and ask who I'm sleeping with at present?' he said bitterly.

Caitlin flushed, stung into anger. Defiantly she raised her chin. 'All right. Who are you sleeping with?'

'No one,' his voice was fierce. 'I've been celibate for months. There, does that make you happy?'

The soft darkness smudged him into shadow. She felt ashamed as he abruptly released her arm, leaving her with a curious sense of desolation. She was bereft.

'You're not wearing an engagement ring yet,' he said. 'That boy-friend of yours is very long-winded.'

Caitlin gave a ghost of a smile. 'He's gone.' She sensed the questioning snap of his head. 'We finally broke up, thanks to you.'

'Me?'

She dragged a toe in the sand. 'He was convinced you and I had had an affair.'

'And he was madly jealous?' Bryce prompted when she offered no further explanation.

Her laugh was cryptic. 'Not really. He became immensely patronising and said he understood. I assured him our friendship was innocent, but basically he didn't care. I realised he'd become a habit, nothing more.'

Bryce reached for her hand which interlaced with his of its own volition. 'I'm glad you've got rid of him.' His fingers tightened on hers. 'Come and have dinner with me this evening, it's time we talked.'

'I can't,' she replied with something approaching relief. 'I'm dining with someone else.'

'Who?' he demanded harshly.

'A man I met on the plane.'

'Oh, Cait.' He swore under his breath. 'Cancel it.'

'No.'

'I've been going crazy waiting for you to arrive,' he mumbled.

Scathingly Caitlin glanced at the dark profile and remembered how rapidly his enthusiasm to contact her had faded. He was acting again, this time playing the ardent lover, but he had conveniently forgotten that he had been too involved with another woman, her cousin, to bother to get in touch. His memory might be hazy, but hers was crystal clear.

'Yes?' she said sarcastically.

'I mean it. The weeks have seemed like years.'

She pulled her hand from his. 'You were perfectly content to allow our friendship to lapse when I returned to London.'

'I can explain that,' he said earnestly.

She tossed her head. 'Don't bother.' All set to walk away, she remembered the interview. Her stomach twisted. She took a deep breath. 'Are you free tomorrow morning? I would prefer to get the interview over as soon as possible.'

'I'm having a day off.' His voice was expressionless. 'I'll pick you up around nine.'

'Fine,' she agreed, and walked determinedly towards the lights of her hotel.

If Chuck had tactfully avoided her she would have understood, but instead he made a beeline for her table the next morning and sat down opposite her, smiling happily. She was acutely aware she had made a poor dinner companion the previous evening, preoccupied as she was with thoughts of Bryce. As she remembered it, the conversation had been vague and fragmented, but either she was a far better actress than she had realised, or Chuck was amazingly insensitive, for he had appeared to notice nothing out of the ordinary.

'Say, what would you say to fishing for blue marlin today?' he suggested, biting into the soft orange flesh of pawpaw.

'Sorry, I can't. I'm booked up. My trip to the Seychelles is to interview an actor, and I shall be seeing him this morning.'

'From the *Slattery* film?'

Her brows raised in surprise. 'Do you have *Slattery* in the States?'

'Not yet, though I understand a series is scheduled to start there soon.' He wiped a trickle of juice from his chin. 'The reason I've heard about it is that I was talking to the receptionist. She says the whole island has been agog for weeks. The filming has been just fantastic. There've been guys leaping from cliffs, hair-raising helicopter rescues, girls in bikinis racing around on huge motorcycles. One of the mountain passes was closed off for a day while the great Slattery himself sliced up and down in a fancy car. Is that the guy you're interviewing?'

Caitlin nodded over the brim of her cup.

'The receptionist reckoned he was something else,' Chuck drawled.

'He is,' she confirmed with a laugh, though her private interpretation of Chuck's phrase was entirely something else, too. She consulted her watch. 'I'd better go. My appointment is for nine.'

He indicated a cheery farewell with a wave of his toast. 'Have a nice day. I'll see you this evening.'

With the flash of a middle-of-the-road smile, Caitlin threaded her way through the tables and out towards her room. She put her small recorder, a supply of fresh batteries, pad and pencils into her straw shoulder bag. With luck the interview would not take long and she would be free to spend the afternoon on the beach, safely away from Bryce. Once the interview was completed there would be no further need to see him again. It was too painful. It was time for their relationship to come to a full stop. Bryce had said he wanted her, but she had no illusions. He wanted her on his own terms—his own selfish masculine terms. No, thank you. She would rather die than join the list of Slattery cast-offs. Joelle was capable of accepting Bryce's short-lived attentions without heartbreak, she was an expert at the throw-away romance herself, but it was not Caitlin's style. If she allowed herself to become further entangled there could be only one consequence— and she preferred not to think about that.

No matter how much she loved him, her pride stopped her from entering into a relationship which she knew was doomed from the start. She wasn't a plaything to keep him happy for a few months until the novelty wore off. She was a woman with needs of her own. Bryce would expect her acquiescence, she thought

wryly. Her willing response to his lovemaking had made
her physical attraction to him clear. But enough was
enough. He must realise she would go no further. In her
head she composed a polite, but firm, ending to their
relationship. The damning sentences were rehearsed
until she was word perfect.

When she opened the door to his knock he was
leaning against the frame, hands slipped into the slit
pockets of casual jeans, thumbs to the fore. He wore a
faded blue sports shirt, unbuttoned to reveal the tangle
of dark hair on his chest. His feet and arms were bare
and brown. Caitlin's treacherous pulses leapt into their
usual frantic dance at the sight of him.

'Get changed,' he ordered, his dark eyes drinking in
her short-sleeved shirtwaister and neat chignon. 'Today
I'm going to show you the island. I have transport, but
it's rather old and grubby. Wear something easy which
won't spoil.'

'What about the interview?'

'You can trot out your questions while we drive,' he
replied smoothly. 'Bring your bikini. There are some
wonderful white-sand beaches, so we'll stop for a swim
somewhere.'

He walked over and sat on the bed, folding his
tanned arms with a decisiveness which brooked no
refusal. 'I'll wait here, hurry up.'

She was too surprised to argue. Meekly she collected
her bikini, shorts and top from a drawer and
disappeared into the bathroom. His command had
caught her off balance, and she submitted to his
instructions, even to the point of unpinning her hair
and brushing it loosely around her shoulders.

'I like it better like that,' he smiled approvingly,
putting both hands behind her neck and weighing the
heavy curls in his palms. His eyes moved down to her
mouth. Caitlin knew he was going to kiss her. She took
a step backwards, but he grasped her shoulders, pulling

her into the prison of his arms. His warm mouth was tentative, questioning against hers and instinctively her lips parted against his. He drew her closer, his kiss deepening as he recognised her answering desire.

'I've missed you so much,' he murmured. 'All these wasted weeks.'

The hypocritical words penetrated, and she wriggled from his grasp. Wasted weeks indeed! Weeks when he had carelessly ignored her existence.

'Let's get going,' she said briskly, slipping on a pair of flat golden sandals which teamed with the light yellow of her towelling top and brief tight shorts. Towels and sunning gear were pushed into her straw bag. Bryce watched thoughtfully. If he was aware she was keeping him at bay he made no comment.

'I rang Joelle at your hotel last night,' she said as they walked out on to the sun-dappled sand of the car park. 'She was out. Do you know where she was?' The searching glance she threw at him belied the casual query.

'No.' His jaw tightened. 'I don't keep tabs on how she spends her time. I hardly know the damn girl.'

'You knew her well enough in Derbyshire,' she replied with a toss of her head.

'We dined together once in a restaurant beneath the gaze of scores of interested onlookers, and there would have been three of us,, only you refused to come,' he said pointedly.

'I had 'flu.'

Hard fingers grabbed her upper arm. Bryce stopped her in her tracks, swinging her round to face him.

'No, you didn't,' he said, his look settling into impatience. 'I don't know what your motives were, but I know damn well you were not ill.'

'It must have been a successful evening.' She blindly ignored his reading of the situation. 'You had great difficulty tearing yourself away from Joelle.'

'Like hell!' he exploded. 'I brought her home at ten-thirty, surely you remember that?'

There was no way Caitlin could confess she had been fast asleep and had only hearsay evidence. She studied the ground, scuffing her toe in the sand.

'I couldn't get away from her quickly enough,' he continued. 'I know she's your cousin and maybe I shouldn't criticise, but she bores me stupid with her giggles and highly spiced gossip.'

Caitlin shifted her shoulders uncomfortably. His words carried the conviction of truth. On reflection it was very possible Joelle had embroidered the facts to give them a fizz of excitement, that was her style. Whispers of an affair with Bryce would raise her reputation among her city friends. She bit her lip reflectively. It seemed she had been hoodwinked.

'You mean you and Joelle weren't . . .' She couldn't bring herself to say 'lovers'. Instead she finished up— 'friendly?'

One black brow arched. 'No chance.'

A battered beach buggy was parked in the shade of a sealing wax palm. As they approached Bryce put his hand in the back pocket of his jeans and produced a key.

'Here we are,' he said, his mouth twitching at her look of astonishment as she examined the car. 'Hardly a Maserati, but perfect for the climate.'

He shot a long leg over the side and swung himself into the driving seat. Many years ago the buggy appeared to have been deep purple, with a gold-sprayed bonnet, but relentless sunshine and salt air had dried the paint into brittleness, and now it was chipped and flaking, revealing large expanses of rusty metal. A flimsy black canvas roof, with several gaping holes, was the only cover.

'What happens when it rains?' she asked, tossing her bag on to the back seat and clambering in beside him.

'You take a hot shower, fully clothed,' he informed her, his eyes brimming with delight.

She giggled. The growing realisation that his evening with Joelle had been entirely innocent, and that the relationship had gone no further, was making her lighthearted. When he put his arm around her shoulders to give her a quick hug, she smiled back happily. He switched on the ignition and they careened out on to the road, Caitlin clinging on to the handrail beside her, for the ride was bumpy. For several minutes they drove along in silence. The road followed the coast, the sea, a gauzy spread of blue, to their left. On the inland side were isolated groups of wooden houses and shops, topped with corrugated iron roofs. Hens and dogs and children played together in the dirt of tiny gardens which clung precariously to the hillsides, for the road was cut into the steep slope of mountains which plummeted down below them to the ocean.

'When do you expect to complete filming?' Caitlin had to raise her voice above the laboured groan of the engine as, with increasing lethargy, the buggy trundled up the gradient towards the headland.

'We hope to have the whole thing in the can in about ten days' time,' Bryce replied, frowning as the engine coughed a protest. 'There are one or two indoor scenes still to be shot, but nothing serious.'

He broke off to jab the gear stick into first, wincing as the engine grated with sour temper. 'Look, let's leave the interview for today, shall we? I'm not in the mood.'

Caitlin chewed at her lower lip and turned from him, staring across the wide blue sea. She had persuaded herself that once the interview was over she would see no more of him, but suddenly she knew that wasn't what she wanted. All the carefully rehearsed lines of farewell were forgotten.

'Fine,' she agreed, casting a sidelong look at him

beneath her lashes. He was whistling through his teeth,
coaxing the best from the reluctant engine, muttering
threats and entreaties. A warm breeze blew the thick
hair straight back from his sunburnt brow. Barefoot in
the casual jeans, he was a different man from Slattery,
far more relaxed and natural. Slattery was a plastic
character, always impeccably groomed, always primed
with glib answers which oozed from his well-shaped lips
like oil.

For several miles the road followed the contours of
the hills. It was edged by stretches of white magnolia
and elephant apple trees, and Caitlin gazed in
fascination at the distant islands and coral reefs
shimmering in the sunshine. Each corner revealed a
view more perfect than the last, seascapes which
appeared to have been plucked from idyllic picture
postcards. The warmth of the tropics invaded her
bones, and she kicked off her sandals and stretched
lazily. The world was beautiful, there was so much to
marvel at and admire.

'What are those?' she asked, pointing up into the
branches of a tree which bore huge prickly-skinned,
green-yellow fruit. They were the size of a football.
Bryce slowed the buggy.

'Durian,' he told her. 'It smells like old socks and
tastes like rotten cream cheese, but it's very popular,
especially in the East. It's supposed to do wonders for
your love life.'

There was a gleam in his eyes which prodded her into
recklessness.

'You'd better steer clear if you're planning to remain
celibate,' she teased.

'I'm not.'

His words sent a torrent of some uncharted emotion
rampaging through her veins, for his black eyes were
scanning her face and she was overwhelmingly aware of
his unspoken meaning. In confusion she avoided his

look, refusing to acknowledge the truth—that he intended to make love to her.

The winding road dropped down to sea level at Port Victoria, the capital town. Its narrow streets were thronged with locals and holidaymakers wandering idly along in the sunshine, pausing to examine shell souvenirs displayed on street-corner stalls, or admiring summer fashions in elegant shop windows. The town was an appealing conglomeration of shanty town and modern architecture, and as they approached the central road junction Caitlin glanced with interest at an ornate silver-painted clock tower.

'It's a replica of one in London,' Bryce said, noticing her look. 'At one time the Seychelles archipelago was a British colony. Earlier the French were in charge.'

'You sound well read.'

'I am,' he agreed with a smile. 'I had nothing to do while I was waiting for you, so I studied the history of the place. The story is fascinating. It stretches back from the slave trade, all the way through to advanced technology. The U.S. Air Force have a satellite tracking station here.'

From the roadside came the babble of an unidentifiable tongue as a hawker extolled the virtues of his produce.

'What is the local language?' she asked.

'A Creole patois.' He drove the buggy into a narrow sidestreet between two tight lines of parked vehicles. 'It's based on French, but has a strong African flavour.'

As he searched for an empty place to park he gave her a potted history of the islands. 'Here we are.' He swung into a gap with only inches to spare. 'Shall we have a look at the market?'

As they walked across the road he casually slipped an arm around her waist and Caitlin found herself relaxing against him as though she had always belonged at his side.

The market place was noisy with laughing and chattering Seychellois of all ages and colours. Caitlin watched them with interest, remembering how Bryce had told her that they had a multi-racial ancestry derived from a vast mix of African, French, Portuguese and British strains. There was a great deal of laughing banter as they bargained for the daily staples of life. A cache of succulent red snapper was surrounded by eager buyers, and for a while Bryce and Caitlin hovered on the fringe of the crowd, watching the cheerful activity. Other stalls were covered with mouthwatering displays of meat, fruit and vegetables—riotous kaleidoscopes of colour—yellow-green pawpaws, the brown-textured crust of pineapples, dark-green avocado pears, creamy bananas and orange mangoes. Curiously they examined an enormous dark brown husk which seemed to consist of two coconuts fused together.

'You like?' A withered old man tapped Caitlin's arm with a bony finger, eager for her attention. When she smiled he grinned back, revealing a shiny wedge of pink gum and a few yellow-stained teeth. They had to concentrate to follow his rapid explanation, in pidgin English, but gathered that the object was called a *coco-de-mer*, a double nut which was highly prized due to its rarity.

'The early travellers, they say it come from tree under the sea,' the old man cackled. He winked at Bryce. 'Good for love. Make her very willing.' He nodded towards Caitlin. 'Make you very strong.' A skinny elbow was thrust into Bryce's ribs by way of confirmation.

'You mean it's an aphrodisiac?' Bryce asked with a grin.

The old man nodded again at Caitlin and rubbed dry palms together, making her blush. 'You buy, you have a happy night.'

'No, thank you,' she said, backing away, struggling

to keep her composure. The old man's leery joy was difficult to resist, and she tugged at Bryce's arm, terrified he might suddenly produce rupees from his pocket and strike a bargain.

'It's a conspiracy against you, Cait,' he smiled as they climbed back into the buggy. 'The Seychelles are a honeymooners' paradise. The air just reeks with love. You'll have to succumb in the end, you know.'

The look in his eyes made her heart somersault.

'Suppose I buy you a durian and a *coco-de-mer*?' he teased. 'That should strip away your inhibitions.'

'I'm not inhibited,' she retorted, as they swung away through the congested streets and out on to the peaceful coast road.

'Then why don't you relax and allow yourself to fall in love with me?'

Her heart caught in her throat.

'I have no intention of becoming just another Slattery girl,' she told him through tight lips.

CHAPTER EIGHT

THE leaden mask of his face stilled any further words. For several minutes Bryce drove on in a furious silence, a silence which barricaded them both behind their own thoughts. When a spit of silver-gilt sand appeared on the seaward side of the road he abruptly wrenched the steering wheel and braked beneath the palms.

'Slattery always crops up, doesn't he?' he said bitterly, fingering the jawline scar. 'And yet you maintain you know the difference between him and me. I wonder if you do.'

Despair knifed through her. 'I do,' she protested, tears springing unbidden into the large hazel eyes. 'I don't like Slattery, but I like you.' She paused, 'I like you a lot, Bryce, but . . .'

'But when I say I want to make love to you, then you consider I'm reverting to Slattery. Is that it?'

She was mesmerised by the rhythmic rub of his forefinger across the jagged white line.

'Yes.' She looked across at him in bewilderment and shook her head. 'No. I mean . . .' With a sob of frustration she covered her face with her hands. 'Oh, I don't know.'

How could she analyse her emotions? She knew she loved Bryce, but where did Slattery fit into it all?

He caught at her hands and firmly pulled them away from her tear-stained face, forcing her to look at him.

'Darling, unless you're prepared to trust me, we'll never get past the Slattery barrier,' he told her softly. 'I trust you. I realise now that when you gave the information about me to the press it was a mistake, and we all make mistakes.'

Snapping up her head, she stared at him. So he still believed she had leaked the news of his departure from the series! She opened her mouth to protest, but Bryce shook his head.

'It's over and done with, Cait. I'm not perfect and I don't expect you to be. I refuse to talk about it again. What matters is how I feel about you. I've missed you like hell since you disappeared overnight in Derbyshire.'

His full mouth twisted into a quick bite of remembered pain. She frowned. Perhaps he really did care. Her thoughts were brushed aside when he gave a diffident shrug.

'But there's no future for us, is there?' he asked. 'I'll always remind you of Slattery, even when he ceases to exist. Hell, he's physically me. We look the same, move the same.' He drew his brows together. 'If only there was some way I could convince you that inside we are two totally different men.'

She swallowed hard to ease the paralysing stiffness in her throat and cast around in her mind for words to explain her fears.

'But you both like women,' she accused, visualising the parade of blondes.

'Naturally, we're red-blooded males,' he said thinly, then added, 'and you like men.'

'That's different.'

'It's not. What about that American guy you dined with last night? You collected him in double-quick time.'

'You're jealous.' Her voice lifted in surprise.

He flushed beneath his tan. 'Yes,' he snapped. 'I was jealous of that boy-friend of yours, as well. Thank goodness you sent him on his way.'

She stared at his glowering face, and began to laugh. Suddenly the world seemed wonderful. Bryce cared, he really cared! She wound her arms coaxingly around his neck and rubbed her nose against his. As his tension evaporated he grinned.

'Let's just enjoy ourselves today, my beautiful Cait.'

When she nodded her agreement he kissed her lightly.

'No more Slattery.' His voice was firm.

'No more Slattery,' she agreed.

The remainder of the morning was spent happily exploring Mahé. They trundled along silver-sand beaches and through the thick vegetation of tropical valleys, until they discovered a small open-air restaurant perched high on a hillside, overlooking a peaceful palm-fringed lagoon. Their table was set beside a trellis of sprawling pink and purple bougainvillaea, and they washed down a tasty prawn curry with tankards of light beer.

'I'm tired, I want to go to sleep,' Caitlin yawned, stretching languidly as they motored back on to the coast. An old wooden sign with faded lettering indicated a track on the seaward side of the road and Bryce swung on to it.

'I think this leads to the bay Frank was telling me about,' he said, as they bounced over the rutted track. 'Apparently it's a couple of miles down to the beach, but it's reputed to be one of the most beautiful on the island, and virtually no one ever comes here.'

There was the glint of aquamarine water between the trees and the white of the sand. Bryce parked in the shade, and then collected their gear and took Caitlin's hand. There was no other sign of human life as they wandered indolently along the edge of the water, dabbling their toes in the surf. Only the gentle thrum of the waves and the whisper of the breeze in the palm trees disturbed the peace. When they reached a tiny private cove at the end of the bay they spread their towels on the fine sand and stripped down to their swimsuits. Caitlin hung her shorts and top on the branches of a flowering bush and then dropped down in the shade. The food and the beer had made her lethargic, and within minutes she dozed off.

The shadows had lengthened when she awoke. Lazily she opened her eyes and lay on her back, admiring the mellow colours of the sky. Bryce was beside her, lying full length, his chin on his hand as he studied her.

She smiled sleepily. 'I'm sorry, I didn't mean to fall asleep.'

'Don't worry. I nodded off too.'

'Have you had a swim?'

He shook his head. 'Too lazy. I've just been lying back, thinking.' He stretched forward and caught a strand of her hair between two fingers. 'Being here has made me realise how pleasant it will be when I'm no longer in the public eye. Most people in the Seychelles don't give a damn about who I am, so they treat me like a normal human being. I like it.' He gave a quick derisive glance at his brief swimming trunks. 'It's a relief not to have to be dressed up like a tailor's dummy all the time. I'm looking forward to being ordinary again.'

'What will you do after the film?' she queried, her eyes meeting his.

'I shan't act for at least two years, and then I intend to completely rethink the situation.' He released her hair to trace the outline of her brows with lazy fingers. 'I've decided to change the emphasis in my life. Instead of acting taking precedence, and the motor business coming second, it will be the other way round. I really do enjoy tinkering with engines, you know. It will be far more satisfying for me, like that. Fame is fine, in small doses, but . . .' his finger trickled across her cheekbone and on to her lips, 'I want to settle down, Cait. Out of the limelight. With you.'

It was as though everything was happening in slow motion. Bryce leaned forward, his eyes on hers, locking her to him until the rest of the world faded from her

consciousness. Now there was only his dark head
blotting out the sun. His lips followed an unswerving
path to hers. Caitlin closed her eyes as she yielded to
the urgent caress of his mouth, the drugging kiss telling
her beyond all doubt of his searing need of her.
Thrusting her arms around his neck, she rubbed the
back of his head, twisting her fingers among the thick
hair with increasing urgency as passion began to claim
her. He dragged his mouth from hers to follow an erotic
path along the sensitive cords of her neck, nibbling and
caressing her. Gently he raised her from the towel, and
she clung to him as he unfastened the top of her bikini.
He pulled it from her and threw it away, resting her
back on the towel.

There was a low animal sound in the back of his
throat as his hands covered her naked breasts. He
moved closer, sliding one leg between her thighs. Caitlin
trembled beneath him, thrusting the swelling curves
deeper into his palms, desperate for his touch on her
nipples. When his fingers caught and teased the winy
peaks she moaned, the wild drumbeat of her heart
pounding against his. Her body was aflame with a fire
she could no longer control.

'I want you,' he muttered raggedly, his hands
surrounding her breasts as his mouth sought the hard
and straining tips. She moaned, her thighs aching for
the rampant maleness of him as she longed for him to
tear away the last remnants of their clothing. When his
hands moved down from her fiery breasts to her waist
she gasped. Dragging her arm tighter around his neck,
she pressed herself against him, exulting in the
roughness of the hairy chest against the sensitivity of
her flesh. Cohesive thought had disappeared, now she
was acting instinctively, a woman with her mate.

'Please, darling, please,' she murmured, suspended
somewhere just out of reach of heaven.

With taut fingers he explored the flat plane of her

stomach, the thrust of her hips, the twin ties of the bikini briefs. Then he sighed and his hands stilled.

'Please, Bryce,' she begged, but his fingers went no further. His weight was pressing her into the sand. Putting her hands against the black sideburns, she raised his head from her and looked questioningly into his eyes. They were dark, heavy with emotion. A nerve twitched in his cheek and she realised the control he was summoning.

'Not here, Cait,' he said thickly. His hands began to move upwards, the fingers splayed in a desire to press against each curve until he had memorised it for ever. Gradually his breathing calmed and she realised the powerful urge had been mastered.

Caitlin didn't know whether to laugh or cry. Instead she gave a soft sigh of frustration.

'I know,' he said, as though she had spoken. 'But not here, my darling, not here on the sand. The first time is too precious for that. We must be alone, somewhere secure.' He glanced towards the line of the bay. 'There's a chance someone could disturb us here.'

He rolled from her to lie at her side, thrusting an arm beneath her shoulders. Tenderly he smoothed the tight skin at her temples.

'I love you, Cait,' he said, then laughed softly as though the novelty of the idea surprised him. 'I really do.'

She turned in his arms and reached up to kiss him. Bryce groaned and as his hand caressed her naked breast his breathing began to quicken again. Caitlin rubbed her hands against the curling dampness of his chest. It felt so wonderful to touch him. She longed to explore the pulsing muscular body without the restriction of clothes.

As though he was reading her mind, Bryce abruptly said, 'Let's go,' and rose from the sand. Putting down two hands he pulled her upright and gathered her against his chest, waiting for a long moment as she recovered from the sensual lethargy he had created. Smiling gently, he picked up her bikini top from the sand and dangled it from one long finger.

'Throw this away,' he teased, his eyes soft with love. 'Be like the other European girls here. Follow fashion and bare all.'

'All?' Her eyes danced with a provocative fire as she glanced at him.

'Perhaps not quite all.' He lifted his brows in a mocking gesture as he studied the brief triangle clinging to her hips. 'That would be more than I could stand.'

His lower lip trembled, warning her that his words were not said in jest. His resistance was low, the humour a fragile façade which scarcely covered the need simmering within him. Calmly she reached out and took the bra top from his finger, bending forward to cup her breasts, then reaching back to fasten the clip. A woman's instinct told her that now it was her responsibility to control the passion between them. Bryce's defences had been shattered.

The knowledge that she could tempt him to make love to her there and then filled her with a feminine delight, and she smiled. She had never seen him so unsure of himself, and he stood mute, watching her every movement as she collected the towels and pulled on her top and shorts. When she handed him his jeans he frowned slightly, but pulled them up on to his hips and tugged at the zip. No words were needed as he claimed her hand and walked back with her across the sand to the buggy.

'We'll go to your hotel.'

She nodded in silent agreement.

The beauty of their surroundings now went unnoticed as they retraced their route along the coast road. Lost in a dream of love, she was only aware of Bryce, though their gaze rarely met. There was no need for the confirmation of her eyes, for already he was with her, their thoughts so entwined that even touch was irrelevant. The journey was the longest, and the shortest, she had ever taken. It passed by in a dream. She was watching a windblown young woman, her lips softly brimming with a secret smile, driving beside a grave young man.

Their arrival at the hotel was a surprise. She had been so engrossed that she was unaware of the passing of time and distance. When they reached her room Bryce hung the 'Do Not Disturb' sign on the outer handle and locked the door.

'I'm sandy,' Caitlin said, in a voice suddenly taut. 'I'll take a shower.'

She was standing beneath the jet of tepid water, soaping herself, when Bryce stepped in behind her. Pulling her backwards from the spray, he buried his face in her shoulder, his hands sliding over her lathered breasts to her hips.

'Oh Cait,' he moaned, 'hurry up, I can't wait for ever.'

As she hurriedly rinsed away the soap bubbles his hands strayed over her glistening body, arousing her until she was hot and her breathing uneven. When they were both dry he lifted her into his arms and carried her to the bed. It felt so right to be held against his hard muscular body. This was where she was destined to belong. Outside, the evening sky was darkly streaked with crimson and grey, but inside, wrapped in the comforting shadows of the room, Caitlin was aware only of the feel and touch of the man beside her.

'I know it's the first time for you, my darling,' he murmured, his lips on her brow. 'I'll try to be gentle.'

The desire which had glowed like an ember since their flight from the beach now burst into flame. Caitlin gave soft gasps of delight as Bryce explored her body, pleasing her until the ache inside her was unbearable.

'I love you,' he said fiercely, his hands moulding her to him as the primitive urge of a man for a woman snared him.

'I love you, too.'

A whirlwind of sensation caught at Caitlin, lifting her skywards as he took her. Her fingertips gripped at his shoulders as she flung back her head in a sharp gasp of pain. Relentlessly he forced her onwards until they both cried out aloud, then she tumbled down, down, down. She was sliding endlessly into a warm dark womb of contentment. Spent with happiness, she lay safely in his arms.

'Did I hurt you?' he asked anxiously.

She smiled, shaking her head. 'It was wonderful,' she assured him.

'And for me, too,' he replied, kissing the fingers which caressed his lips. 'I never knew it could feel like this. There's always been something missing, but with you . . .' He buried his face in her neck. 'Love makes all the difference,' he muttered, and his mouth claimed hers again.

Slowly the passion rose between them, blossoming beyond belief as they re-explored each other's body. This time their love was relaxed and languorous. Each kiss, each caress was savoured to the full. But the delicious outcome was inevitable as their limbs moved and their breathing quickened.

Much later Bryce lifted a heavy arm and looked at his watch in the lamplight.

'I'll have to leave, darling. It's gone eleven.' He nuzzled at the curls around her temples. 'I wish I could stay with you all night, but there's a six o'clock call in the morning. If I don't return to my hotel and get some sleep I shall look very haggard tomorrow.'

She snuggled deeper into his arms. 'Slattery never looks haggard,' she teased.

He laughed and gently pulled his arm away. 'He will,

if I don't get some sleep, and if I stay here with you, there's no way I shall waste time sleeping.'

He reached for his jeans with a reluctant sigh. 'I must go, but I promise you once the film is finished we'll be together all night and all day.' He bent to kiss her. 'Go to sleep, Cait. The best sleep always comes afterwards.'

She sighed. Dimly she heard the door close, and then she floated away on a cotton-wool cloud of contentment.

When she awoke she smiled, hugging the ecstasy of the night before to her like a blanket. Stretching lazy arms, she climbed out of bed and pulled on a robe. Bright sunlight flooded the- room when she opened the curtains, and she blinked. There was a sheet of notepaper beside her watch on the bedside table.

'Will phone after filming—around six. Sweet dreams, my love. Bryce.'

The day would drag. She wished it was evening already. Ruefully she wondered if his snatched hours of sleep had been sufficient. The camera was ruthless in detecting telltale shadows of tiredness, or unflattering lines. Slattery always looked in prime condition, as though he had just walked out from a fortnight at a health farm. She grinned, taking perverse satisfaction in the knowledge that if the private detective was a little below par that morning, it was entirely her fault.

After showering she pulled on white cotton trousers and a floral green and gold Hawaii-style shirt. 'Take that stupid grin off your face,' she told her reflection in the mirror, but it was impossible. Bryce's track record with the Slattery girls no longer mattered. All she needed was his love, and she had that. It was enough to live for the moment, indulging herself with thoughts of the lovemaking they had shared, and would share again soon. Worries about the future could be left to another day.

Chuck beckoned as she entered the restaurant, leaving her no alternative but to join him at his table.

'I missed you yesterday evening,' he said, with a look of reproach. 'Were you tied up with that actor?'

Caitlin nodded, bending her head to concentrate on unwrapping the foil from a cube of butter. She was not ready yet to talk about Bryce. The knowledge of their shared love was too new to be bandied around in public.

'You rate him?' Chuck asked archly, noticing her quiet withdrawal. There was a sharp questioning edge to his voice as though he disapproved.

'Highly,' she confirmed with an inward smile at the drawled expression.

'I was wondering if you wanted to see something of the island today,' he muttered, 'now I guess you'll be occupied.'

'I'm not. But to be honest, it is serious between Bryce and me.'

He scowled at the other holidaymakers in the restaurant.

'There's no one else I dig.'

Privately Caitlin thought some of the unattached girls were very pretty, but he was not to be distracted.

'So how about it? Suppose we visit the tea plantation? I've never seen tea grown before, have you?'

'No. It would be interesting,' she admitted. Her mind swung like a yo-yo in indecision. Perhaps it would be prudent to spend the day on the beach. Bryce might not approve if she accompanied Chuck. And yet as she might never visit the Seychelles again, it seemed pointless to miss the opportunity of investigating the local life.

'We can order packed lunches and have a picnic,' Chuck coaxed.

'I don't know,' she demurred.

'We'd be back early. Hell, it's the one and only time

I'm ever likely to be here, and it's no fun on your own.'

'True,' she conceded. Sightseeing was innocuous enough. Surely Bryce would not object to her visiting a tea plantation, even if it was with another man?

'Great, that's settled,' the American said firmly, brushing aside her doubts. With breathtaking efficiency he arranged a hire car, collected packed lunches, cans of lager and lemonade, and worked out their route. His enthusiasm was infectious, and she had to concede he was good company. He drove along, chattering non-stop. Each view reminded him of some anecdote, and Caitlin was soon shaking with laughter at his tall stories. The day which she had imagined would drag began to sparkle.

They followed a mountain road across the backbone of Mahé, dropping down between lush fields to the tea plantation. At the gates they joined a guided tour, and walked through the fields, listening to a commentary of how the tea bushes were tended. Next stop was the factory. Chuck spent all his time taking photographs, and Caitlin was required to pose in front of tea chests, beside the machinery, and with the dark-skinned girls who were busily packing the dried leaves.

'They'll love these back in Flagstaff,' he crowed, leaping around, jabbing at light meters, working out distances and correct exposures. The tour guide eyed him with unconcealed amusement. Afterwards they sampled different blends of tea in a small garden café adjoining the factory, and then set off again in the car, the windows wound down to allow the warm sultry breeze to circulate.

'This must be where the wealthy guys live,' Chuck commented as they followed the steep upward curve of the road through forested hillsides. Elegant villas were briefly visible through the trees, and they passed several imposing gateways, guarded with stone lions and sentry boxes. As they rounded a bend Chuck braked suddenly.

The narrow road was blocked, thronged with men,
women and children all peering through black wrought
iron gates towards a distant house at the end of a long
drive.

'I wonder what's happening here?' he said, drawing
to a halt on the grass verge. 'Must be something
exciting.'

'Whatever it is, the locals are interested,' Caitlin
commented, 'Apart from the guards!'

Two Negroes in grubby tee-shirts and shorts were
lounging just inside the gates, eyes half closed,
seemingly immune to the excited chatter of the crowd.

'I wouldn't fancy my chances if they were guarding
me,' Chuck laughed.

Suddenly a large white limousine appeared from the
direction of the house, and the guards sprang to life,
officiously waving back the crowd as they rushed
forward, swinging open the gates. There was a murmur
as the car purred out on to the road. Everyone swivelled
to watch its progress. As it passed them there was a
glimpse of a blonde head and Caitlin clutched Chuck's
arm.

'That's my cousin Joelle,' she said delightedly. 'She's
an actress, and has a part in the *Slattery* film. This must
be the villa where the film is being produced.'

'Gee, do you think we could have a look inside?' he
asked. 'I've never seen a movie being shot. It would be
great if I could take some snaps. My mom would be
real thrilled to know I'd been on a set.'

'Frank Stern, the director, probably wouldn't
welcome unannounced visitors,' Caitlin said slowly.

The two guards had closed the gates again, and were
lolling back once more on the stone gateposts, eyelids
drooping.

'Film making is a serious business,' she continued,
'and he isn't the most agreeable of men.'

'But surely you're here in a professional capacity as a

journalist?' Chuck pressed. 'The guy must want publicity for his film. You work for a widely read magazine, so you'll be providing it. He could have no objection to your visiting the set to obtain more details for your article.'

Caitlin frowned. A wider knowledge of the background of the film would be useful when she wrote up the interview with Bryce. No matter how much he told her, the account would have an added richness if she, herself, had seen him at work. She would be able to include authentic touches which would lift the writing.

'I suppose there's no harm in asking at the gate if visitors are allowed,' she said, chewing her lip. She was reluctant to intrude. If Bryce had wanted her to watch him filming, doubtless he would have invited her.

Chuck ignored the indecision on her face and picked up his camera. 'That Slattery guy will be delighted to see you,' he said confidently, leaping from the car.

Caitlin was not convinced. Bryce took his acting very seriously and her presence was bound to disrupt the flow of action. She looked at her watch, it was noon. Perhaps the film crew would have stopped work for a few minutes.

Chuck put out a hand. 'Come on.'

'Let's keep a low profile,' she suggested, allowing herself to be pulled towards the guards. Dubiously the two men listened as she explained her position as a member of the British press. They exchanged doubtful looks until Chuck produced a handful of notes, and then they smiled broadly and decided between themselves that there was no harm if the young couple visited the set. The gates were pulled back to allow them to slide through.

She made mental notes on the large white house as they walked up the drive towards it. Built in a clearing among the trees, it was on two storeys. Wild bougainvillaea and blossoms she was unable to identify grew in profusion on its walls, twining around the pillars which supported a terrace stretching the full width of the ground floor. There was a tiled patio and shimmering swimming pool to one side, while outhouses and garages were on the other. It was a luxurious spread. The front door stood open, and there were signs of activity within. On the gravel drive before the house were scaffolds, boxes, parked cars, and as they approached a loudspeaker bayed out something unintelligible. There was a sudden rush of people from the front door of the house out into the driveway, and they quickly dispersed, some gathering around the cars, others sprawling out on the grass in the sunshine. Several walked towards the pool.

'Must be lunchtime,' Chuck announced, and she began to relax a little. Presumably there could be no objection to their presence during a break. They were not interrupting the work. She glanced around, hoping to see Bryce, but without success. Frank Stern was leaning against a car, eating a sandwich, chatting idly to a second man.

Caitlin took a deep breath and stepped forward, Chuck at her side. 'Hullo, Mr. Stern,' she smiled pleasantly. 'Remember me? I'm Caitlin Saunders. I interviewed Bryce in Derbyshire, and my magazine has sent me over here to interview him again.'

Abruptly the director left his companion and took a step towards her. 'Get the hell off my set,' he said coldly. He jerked his head at Chuck. 'We don't want intruders.'

The ferocity of his manner surprised her, and Caitlin flushed.

'Don't you allow the press on location?' she asked.

'I don't mind the press in general, but,' he jabbed a finger in her direction, 'I damn well don't want *you*.'

'My article will be read by millions of women in the

U.K.,' she pointed out. 'It will be excellent publicity for your film.'

'I'm well aware of that,' Frank snapped. 'But Bryce doesn't want you here. We have enough trouble with women drooling over him as it is.'

His voice was fierce, and their argument was drawing the attention of several technicians who were watching from the sidelines. In embarrassment Caitlin lowered her head. She caught a sudden movement in the corner of her eye as Chuck leaned towards the director.

'Cool it, man,' he ordered, glaring down at the bald head.

Casually Frank brushed a crumb from the side of his mouth. 'Bryce gave implicit instructions that this young woman was not to be allowed anywhere near him.'

Pain, like a granite claw, clutched at Caitlin's heart. Something in Frank's smug satisfaction told her he was telling the truth. He leaned back on his heels with the air of someone who had delivered a master stroke.

'This lady is his special girl,' Chuck said by way of explanation.

'They *all* think they're his special girl,' Frank sneered.

The American flexed his shoulders threateningly, his face darkening. Caitlin put an anxious hand on his arm.

'Let's go.'

Her plea was ignored.

'That guy's asking for trouble,' he told her, looming over the director like Goliath over David. He put his hands on his hips and said in a loud voice, 'We demand to speak to Cameron.'

'This is my film set and I'm in charge here,' Frank retorted angrily, refusing to be intimidated. 'Bryce doesn't want her around, that's all there is to it.'

Several other members of the crew were drifting across to listen to the quarrel. Caitlin eyed them warily.

'Let's leave, Chuck.'

'Yes, why don't you?' Frank sneered. 'Everything

was going along fine until you cropped up.'

Chuck raised two massive fists. 'You're a real pain in the ass, mister. This is no way to treat a lady. You just go and tell that Cameron guy we want to see him.'

A thousand panic-stricken butterflies charged around Caitlin's stomach. Frank's unwelcoming attitude was far more severe than she had ever expected, and Chuck's refusal to let matters rest was aggravating the situation even further.

'Bryce is at lunch,' the director told them heavily. 'He's been filming for the past three hours. I don't intend to have him disturbed.'

'The lady only wants to see him for five minutes,' Chuck threatened.

'I don't,' she squeaked, her face flaming. 'Please, let's go.'

'No way.' The American was like a dog worrying at a bone, determined not to release his grip. 'If the guy's at lunch, then we're not interrupting.' He leaned towards Frank. 'He'll want to see his fiancée.'

'I'm not his fiancée,' she inserted quickly, but she was not quick enough.

Frank pounced on the word. 'Fiancée, is it?' he asked. His eyes skimmed round the watching audience, inviting them to join in his fun. 'That's a new description!'

A titter of laughter rippled around as Frank smirked. Anger lifted Caitlin's chin, and her eyes widened as Bryce suddenly came through the front door of the villa and sauntered towards them. He was wearing a black leather suit which fitted like a second skin. The jacket was unzipped halfway down his chest and a heavy gold medallion swung against the crisp black hairs. He looked supremely male and vital, and all eyes swung to monitor his progress. Her pulses juddered at the sight of him and then she smiled. Rescue was at hand.

He stopped a yard from her. 'Go away, Caitlin,' he

said quietly. 'Go away. I don't want you here. I'll see
you this evening.' His expression was solemn and
forbidding. She stared at him in astonishment and
dismay, unable to believe her ears. Last night he had
held her close and told her that he loved her, and now
. . . Everyone was watching his rejection of her, and
reaching their own conclusions. In misery she bent her
head. There was no sign of love on his face, no warmth,
no affection. He was steel, through and through; cold,
hard steel. He was agreeing with Frank's assessment of
her, that she was merely another drooling woman. He
did not want her here. He did not give a damn about
her feelings. He was one hundred per cent Slattery.
Slattery who kissed and dismissed.

With a burning face she pivoted on her heel and
marched back to Chuck. 'We're going,' she snapped,
closing her fingers possessively around his arm in an
attempt to salvage what dignity she could. The
onlookers were silent. Chuck frowned and looked
across at Bryce.

'But I thought you and he . . .' he began.

'You thought wrong,' she ground out icily, pulling
him with her down the drive with ever increasing paces,
'and so did I.'

The interested eyes of the film crew hooked into her
back as they retreated down the drive. She had never
felt so humiliated in her life. Then she corrected herself.
Another humiliation was firmly engraved on her soul—
when Bryce had given her the dud interview. For a
moment she faltered in her race. It would serve him
right if she went back and lashed at that handsome face
of his, but the thought of the leering crowds stopped
her. The film crew would be as greedily interested in
Bryce's private life as the villagers in Derbyshire.

At last they reached the gates and life-saving
anonymity. She clenched her teeth determinedly as they
pushed through the locals on to the road, but as soon as

they reached the safety of the car her composure snapped and she began to sob.

For several minutes Chuck held her close against his plaid shirt.

'Don't cry, honey,' he implored, gazing down at her tearful face. 'I guess he's unreliable. Actors are like that.'

'I thought he loved me,' she wept, twisting away to scrub furiously at her eyes with a sodden tissue. 'But I was just another of his girls. If he really cared he would never have sent me away.'

'Put it down to experience,' Chuck suggested in an attempt to comfort her. 'Not all men are such slobs.'

'I suppose not,' she gulped, blowing her nose loud and long. 'I hate Bryce Cameron. He needn't think he can fool me again!'

'Good girl,' he said encouragingly. He watched as she wiped her wet cheeks, tossed away her tissue and turned to flash him a smile which started off as brilliant, but wobbled in the middle.

'I'm better now,' she assured him. 'Shall we go to the beach and have lunch?'

With a relieved glance at her resolute expression he started the car. 'Yes, ma'am,' he smiled.

For the rest of the day she sparkled defiantly, thrusting aside memories of Bryce's treachery, for she knew that if she allowed herself to dwell on his behaviour she would burst into tears again. If Chuck suspected her bright smiles and friendly camaraderie sprang from weak roots, he never commented but tactfully avoided further reference to the scene at the villa. He entered wholeheartedly into her mood, laughing and joking, entertaining her with the skill of a court jester.

The hotel had provided a delicious picnic of chicken drumsticks, salad, cheese and fresh fruit, and after doing it justice they sunbathed. Later came a long frolic in the sea, and it was almost seven o'clock when they returned to Beau Vallon Bay. Caitlin gave the receptionist explicit instructions that any callers were to be firmly advised that she was out.

When Chuck suggested that they dine together and go on to the hotel disco, she accepted readily. Damn Bryce, she rebelled, as she showered and changed. He had made her fall in love with him, but she had never worked through the implications. It was obvious he would expect her to behave like one of the Slattery girls. Obeying his whims, falling in with his plans, being on call when he wanted, and keeping out of the way when he wanted that, too. But she was not a robot, programmed to suit his needs. She refused to be picked up and discarded.

The gold lurex jumpsuit she chose to wear for her evening with Chuck was cut dangerously low at the front. After revealing the fullness of her cleavage, it hugged her waist, then clung to the smooth curves of her hips and thighs. In the past she had wondered if it was too provocative for comfort, but this evening it seemed exactly right. Her confidence had been badly bruised. Masculine approval was what she hungered for, and the golden jumpsuit would provide it.

Her make-up was flawless. Gold shadow shimmered on her lids, while a carefully applied whisper of kohl around her large eyes gave them a mysterious dominance in the smoothness of her complexion. Her lips were outlined with dark-rose gloss and carefully filled in with a paler shade, making the lips she pursed at the mirror moist and tempting. After a liberal spray of French perfume she slipped her feet into high golden sandals and stared aggressively at her reflection. Looking sexy made her feel good.

Male heads turned comfortingly to examine her outline in the clinging outfit as she made her way across the lobby. She raised her chin, meeting the blatant admiration with flashing eyes. It was a heady feeling, being a desirable woman, and knowing it.

'Wow!' Chuck gasped, his eyes nearly popping out of his head when she joined him. 'You've certainly got your act together this evening!' As his eyes slid down her cleavage she tossed back the cloud of chestnut curls and breathed deeply. 'Wow,' he said again in awe.

She flirted outrageously with him throughout the meal, and drank far more wine than usual. Once, when a tall dark-haired man appeared in the entrance to the restaurant, her provocative charade stilled, but he turned into the light and she realised he was a stranger. Her heart plummeted. For a moment she was tempted to abandon her performance and rush for the dark privacy of her room, but Chuck reached for her hand. Another defiant gulp of wine, and she mentally sent Bryce skidding off to hell.

The disco was in full swing when they arrived. Loud music and flashing lights removed any need for conversation, and Caitlin was grateful. Chuck was a good dancer, and she abandoned herself to the hypnotic tempo. The wine had loosened her inhibitions and she gyrated before him, swinging her goldenly shimmering hips in a deliberate display of her sexuality. With pouting lips and glittering dark eyes she flaunted herself. Bryce might reject her, but she knew Chuck never would. Her hazel eyes flashed with the promise of delights to come, and as the lights tinted her skin from green to magenta to bronze, she dipped and swayed to the latest reggae beat.

'You're the sexiest thing I ever saw,' said Chuck, close to her ear. She raised her brows provocatively, then suddenly a steel claw shot out of nowhere and encircled her arm.

'Stop it!' a voice thundered over the drugging beat of the music. 'Stop it, Caitlin! You're mine, not his.'

CHAPTER NINE

BRYCE stood motionless before her, anger tightening the skin across his cheekbones. She stopped dancing and put her hands on her hips.

'Don't shout at me!' she flared. 'I'm nobody's possession. I belong to myself. I do *what* I like, *when* I like and *how* I like!'

The black eyes were glassy with emotion, freezing through her fever, thawing it instantly. Caitlin gave an involuntary shudder. The intoxication of the wine drained as his fingers tightened, biting into her flesh until she gave a wordless gasp of pain. Abruptly he swung away, striding through the crush of dancers, dragging her with him.

'Let me go!' She desperately pulled at his fingers in an attempt to prise them from her arm.

'I won't have you behaving so, so . . .' his voice cracked, 'so damn wantonly with other men,' he finished. 'You're mine and I love you.' His eyes were hard and hurt.

'I'm not yours,' she retorted, but it fell on stony ground.

His pace increased until she was almost running beside him. He propelled her towards the entrance where he was forced to pause at the swing doors to allow another couple to enter. The brief delay gave Chuck time to gather his wits and make chase. Pushing his way across the crowded dance floor, he joined them, large fists clenched at the ready.

'For heaven's sake, don't fight,' she pleaded, as Bryce twisted round to face the tall American, his face pale with rage. Her arm was released as he prepared to attack, and distractedly Caitlin rubbed at the fiery imprint of his fingers, her heart in her mouth, as she watched the two men. Height for height they were equally matched. Like two snarling dogs they confronted each other, reflexes quivering, waiting for a weakness to reveal itself before hurling themselves into the fray.

'Leave her alone,' Chuck snapped.

'Why the hell should I?' Bryce countered. 'She's my girl.'

The American's nostrils flared in derision. 'Yeah?' he drawled, and as he lunged Caitlin flung herself on his arm, deflecting the blow destined for Bryce's jaw. For a second Chuck faltered, thrown off balance.

'Keep out of this, Cait,' Bryce ordered, pushing her safely aside. 'You'll be hurt.' He flexed his shoulders, eyeing the American with intense dislike.

'Don't be so stupid!' she cried. 'You're making fools of yourselves!' She pivoted. 'I'm going. I'm taking no part in this disgusting display of senseless aggression!'

The words sounded very grand, but inside was a frightened little girl, for deep down she recognised that the entire blame for the situation lay on her shoulders. Wildly she pushed open the swing doors and rushed outside, running down the steps and across the wide lawns surrounding the pool. As she turned into the hotel lobby there was the sound of footsteps behind her. Her pulse tripped in fear. Desperately she increased her pace, but the golden heels were far too high for speedy retreat. She bent down and tugged them off, dangling them from her fingers as she ran, pell-mell, in bare feet along the corridor. The footsteps were catching up. When she reached her room she pulled the key from her purse and thrust it into the lock. Her heart was pounding in her ears as she heaved open the door, stepped inside, and slammed it shut behind her. The footsteps grew to a crescendo, and her breath caught in her throat when they stopped outside her room.

'I must speak to you, Cait.' In his agitation the Scots accent thickened the words as Bryce's request came low and firm to her ears.

'Go away.' Her voice was weak. She cleared her throat. 'Go away!' The demand was stronger the second time.

'We must talk. I can explain everything.'

'Go away!' Hysteria splintered in her throat and she put a shaking hand to her brow. The skin was red hot.

'Caitlin, my darling, I'm sorry about today.' There was a pause. 'Look, I can't talk to you like this,' he said reasonably. 'I'll disturb the other guests. For heaven's sake, open the door.'

Biting on her lip, she turned away from the appeal. 'No!'

'Please, darling.' His desperation was clear enough, but Caitlin hardened her heart. Pretence was his profession, something at which he was an expert. She put her fists to her temples.

'Go away,' she implored. Suddenly hot salty tears were pricking in her eyes, turning the door into a blurry mass. 'Go away, *Slattery!*'

His stony withdrawal pummelled at her senses, although it was invisible to her. Seconds later there came the snap of his footsteps on the stone stairs, and then the muffled hum of a rapidly retreating vehicle. As Caitlin flung herself on the bed the tears began to flow. When the first rash was spent, there came harsh racking sobs, until eventually those stopped, too. She was cried out and exhausted, but it was late in the night before the relief of sleep rescued her from her misery.

An anxious enquiry at reception the following morning revealed that Chuck had disappeared for the day on a fishing trip. Relieved that he had suffered no major ill effects from his confrontation with Bryce, she made her way out on to the sun terrace, feeling thankful for small mercies. It was bad enough that she was suffering, but Chuck had wandered innocently between her and Bryce, and there was no reason why he should be hurt.

Stretched out on a sunlounger, she spent the morning drifting numbly between sleep and stale thought. Her pulses throbbed in anguish. Bryce would be unwilling to allow their relationship to die, she knew that, but die it must, no matter how painful the consequences. He had already proved himself capable of tearing her apart, and this was only the beginning. She could not stay around to take any more hurt. Despairingly she twisted over on to her stomach and rested her head on her hands. Her spirits swooped downwards as she realised there was the interview to be considered. It was the reason for her visit. Alison would have her hanged, drawn and quartered if she returned to London empty-handed. Her career would be on the line, so like it, or not, she was forced to see Bryce again. The meeting was bound to be fraught with problems, but her professional life took precedence.

It was early afternoon before she could summon up sufficient composure to set the wheels in motion. With a trembling hand she lifted the receiver to contact his hotel. Bryce would be absent filming, but she had decided to take the initiative and arrange an appointment.

'I'd like to leave a message for Mr Cameron,' she told the girl on the switchboard.

'Mr Cameron is in hospital.'

For a deadening moment her senses malfunctioned. 'I beg your pardon?' The query was weak, her legs suddenly shaking.

'He had an accident while he was filming.' The voice over the telephone was impersonal.

Caitlin's hand flew to her throat. 'What happened? Is he badly hurt?'

The daredevil stunts with cars and helicopters flashed vividly through her mind. He had had car accidents before. The scar on his jaw was a legacy from a nasty smash.

'Apparently it's his legs. I'm afraid I have no further information.' The girl was anonymously efficient. 'What message would you care to leave? Naturally I am unable to guarantee a reply. I have no idea if he will be returning to the hotel.'

'No message,' she said faintly, putting the receiver back into the cradle. Her head dropped into her hands. She had presumed Bryce was filming at the villa, but some last-minute retake must have cropped up and he had ventured out again on one of his breathtaking escapades. Caitlin groaned. He had told her how dangerous some of the stunts could be, how they required split-second timing. All it needed was a slight miscalculation and then—disaster! Re-lifting the telephone, she gnawed at her lip as she waited for the girl to come on the line.

'Could you put me through to the hospital?' she asked.

'Which hospital, ma'am?'

Oh dear, she hadn't realised there would be more than one.

'The main hospital.' It was a blind guess.

'Certainly, ma'am.'

There was a click as the girl deserted her to make the call. The waiting minutes were like years. She gave a sigh of relief when there came a second click.

'Good afternoon, General Hospital here.'

'I believe a Mr Bryce Cameron has been admitted,' she babbled. 'Please could you tell me his condition?'

'Cameron? Cameron?' The voice trailed off. 'Wait a minute. I'll check the admissions register.'

Her fingers clammy around the receiver, Caitlin waited. In the background she heard the woman call to someone else, there was mumbling and then silence. Her anxiety grew.

'I understand Mr Cameron is in the coronary unit at present,' the voice said at last.

Grunting an agonised 'Thank you', she put down the telephone and quickly started to change. Coronary unit! His condition must be critical. She dressed in a loose cotton-voile smock of lemon and white, with shoestring straps on each shoulder. Rapidly brushing back her hair into a ponytail, she tied it with a matching scarf, leaving the ends to waft freely across her shoulders. She grabbed her bag and ran down to the hotel entrance. A taxi was waiting in the shade of a bamboo thicket and she wrenched open the door, flinging 'General Hospital, please' at the driver.

'How can he drive so slowly?' she fretted as she sat tightly on the back seat, knees together, hands gripped in her lap. The taxi driver was friendly, he had an eye for a pretty girl and was eager to chat, but try as she might Caitlin found it impossible to respond naturally. She nibbled at her fingers, and urged the taxi along, as though her own strength of will would make the wheels turn faster. At last they stopped outside a long, low, whitewashed building.

'General Hospital, miss,' the driver smiled.

She pulled two notes from her purse.

'Sorry, miss, I got no change. You wait here, I go find some.'

'No, no, take it all.' She thrust the notes into his hand and climbed out. He looked down at them and grinned. Bonanza!

'I wait here, take you back,' he offered happily.

Her smile was uncertain. 'I don't know how long I shall be.' If Bryce's condition was critical then she was prepared to keep a vigil for hours, days, weeks.

'I wait,' he said reassuringly. Even if the remainder of the afternoon was spent parked in the hospital grounds, he would still make a profit, and why bother to work when he was in funds!

She nodded her thanks and walked quickly into the tiled entrance hall. 'Could I see Mr Cameron, please?' she asked the girl behind the counter. 'I understand he's in the coronary unit.'

The girl consulted a list. 'He's left there now,' she said brightly. 'At present he is being examined in the blood unit. I'm afraid no one can see him.'

Her heart quaking, Caitlin clung to the edge of the counter. 'How badly hurt is he?' She tried to control her fear, but it was galloping away.

'We don't know yet, miss. He is still under observation. There are a series of tests to be made before the doctors can issue a report. The results should be through in two to three hours. Naturally no one can see him until they are completed. I suggest you come back then.'

She hesitated, thrown into blind confusion. Should she wait at the hospital, or return to the hotel? Through the open door she caught a glimpse of the taxi driver still waiting outside in the sunshine. He raised his hand in a friendly salute as she looked towards him. She sighed. If she waited here, sat on the hard wooden bench at the side of the hall, she would go to pieces. Far better to return to the hotel and come back later, at least the drive to and fro would kill some intervening time.

It was only when she was back in her room again that she began to have doubts. Perhaps it would have been wiser to wait at the hospital. She paced the room, then lifted the telephone.

'General Hospital, please.' Her voice was tight. Blood unit, coronary unit? And the girl at his hotel had said Bryce's legs were injured. Despairingly she shook her head.

'Could you give me the latest news on Mr Cameron?' she asked when the hospital came on the line.

'An ambulance has taken him back to his hotel. There's no more we can do for him.'

At the last sentence she swayed. It sounded like a death knell. Relinquishing the telephone she ran down to the lobby, but the taxi had disappeared. For several frustrating minutes she waited, hoping another one would arrive, but when there was no sign of activity she abandoned the idea, and decided it would be quicker to walk along the beach to Bryce's hotel. Hooking off her sandals, she walked down the sand to where it was firm and sea-washed at the water's edge. The burn of the tropical sun on her bare arms and legs went unnoticed as she strode towards the distant palm trees. His hotel was a sprawling complex set in lush gardens overlooking the beach and wide throw of the Indian Ocean. Guests were luxuriously housed in individual bungalows built of wood and thatched with faded brown attap. The architect had sited each a discreet distance from its neighbour, amidst burgeoning bougainvillaea and clumps of palms. Fragrance from colourful blossoms drifted on the balmy breeze.

Flushed from her rapid walk, Caitlin left the beach as the first bungalows came into view and followed the narrow cobbled path which meandered between them. The grounds were deserted. Guests would be stretched out on the sand or busy sightseeing. She looked around in dismay, and started to make for the main building of the hotel in the distance. When she heard the sudden clunk of a door closing she pivoted. A plump dark-skinned woman, in the starched white of a nurse's uniform, had exited from a bungalow to her far left. Quickly she veered.

'Excuse me,' she panted as the woman paused. 'I'm looking for Mr Cameron. I understand he's had an accident. I wondered if you knew where I could find him?'

The woman folded her arms across her stiff bosom and smiled.

'This is Mr. Cameron's bungalow, the ambulance brought him back twenty minutes ago.' She nodded her head at the door behind her. 'I've settled him into bed and he's resting right now. I'm off to have a cup of coffee, there's no more I can do at present. In an hour or two I'll be back to serve him his dinner.'

'Do you think I could see him?'

'I don't see why not. Be quiet, though, he may be asleep.'

As the woman walked away Caitlin pushed open the door and stepped inside. The bungalow was expensively furnished. It was a self-contained unit with lounge, tiny bar and kitchenette, one bedroom and en-suite bathroom. The bedroom door was ajar, the room shadowy, curtains closed to cut out the glare of the sun. For a moment she waited, allowing her eyes to become accustomed to the gloom, then she tiptoed forward, her heart in her mouth.

Bryce was in bed, the sheets pulled up neatly to his chest, his bare shoulders gleaming in the dim light. His arms lay rigidly at his sides on the beige coverlet. Caitlin took a tentative step further into the room. The covers at the foot of the bed were raised, outlining some kind of contraption to protect his legs. For a stricken moment her head throbbed with scenes of mangled limbs, bones protruding through flesh, Bryce trapped in a wrecked car, or falling like a rag doll on to merciless rocks. Pushing the back of her hand against her lips to stifle a sob, she crept towards the bed.

He was fast asleep, his breathing slow and deep. Hesitantly she perched herself on the edge of the bed and inspected him. The strong arms and shoulders were unmarked, and his face showed no sign of injury. She gave a sigh of relief. Tenderly she stretched out her hand and pushed aside the dark fall of hair from his brow.

'Oh, Bryce, I love you so much,' she murmured. Her voice broke over the choking lump in her throat. 'I'll look after you, my darling.' Her eyes travelled down to the raised bedclothes over his legs. 'No matter what's happened, I'll spend my life caring for you.'

She traced the glossy thickness of a sideburn with her finger, then the movement faltered as one heavy lid was slowly raised, and then the other. Laughing eyes surveyed her. In astonishment she gazed at him as a grin spread across his full mouth.

'You fraud!' She sat bolt upright. 'You weren't asleep at all!'

He reached out and pulled her towards him until she collapsed on to his chest and his plundering mouth covered hers, snatching away her words of relief and amazement. Caitlin pushed herself free.

'What's happened?' she asked in bewilderment. 'Is your heart okay? What's the matter with your legs? Are they broken?'

She noticed the masculine amusement on his face and arched a suspicious brow. He certainly didn't resemble a man on the brink of death.

'The hotel receptionist said you'd had an accident while you were filming. I've been to the hospital, but they wouldn't let me see you.' Suddenly her eyes were brimming with tears. 'Oh Bryce, it was terrible! I thought you had been badly injured.'

He held her against his chest, stroking her hair.

'Darling, darling,' he soothed. 'I'm fine. I'm sorry you've been upset.'

'Upset!' she muttered. 'I've been to hell and back!'

Bryce pushed the pillow behind him and carefully edged up the bed until he was leaning upright against it. He opened his arms and Caitlin nestled against him. Gently he kissed her brow, whispering words of comfort. She turned to view the cage at the foot of the bed.

'But what have you done?'

'I fell off a step,' he admitted, his lips moving into a wry smile. 'I've sprained my ankle, that's all.'

Relief flooded through her. She didn't know whether to laugh or cry.

'A step—one step?' she asked in disbelief.

'One lousy step,' he confirmed. 'Sorry, I couldn't even manage to fall down a full flight.' His grin was self-deprecating. 'I was standing in the doorway of the villa, arguing with Frank. Our conversation became rather fast and furious. I swung away in disgust, overbalanced and ended up flat on my back. Most embarrassing!' He lowered his eyes.

She began to giggle. 'That doesn't sound much like . . .' She intended to say Slattery, but she stopped and changed her mind. 'Like you,' she finished.

With startling clarity she realised Slattery was no longer important. Bryce was not Slattery, he merely acted out the character. When she recalled the past she realised that there had been an avalanche of clues to indicate, beyond all doubt, that Bryce was his own man. Her mind switched to the 'mental swagger'. He used it when it was expected of him, when he was on view as the millionaire detective. The image was contrived, a public relations exercise, carefully calculated to drum up an expected response. And it had been ruthlessly effective. For a long time she had been deceived, half believing him to hold the same values as Slattery, but now . . .

Bryce was so different. Tender, thoughtful, loving. She smiled. Physically the man she loved was identical to Slattery, but emotionally he was entirely different.

Her eyes swivelled to the foot of the bed.

'Is it serious?'

'No.'

He stretched his lower lip in a gesture of rueful disgust. 'Frank overreacted. As soon as he saw me lying on the ground in front of him, he panicked. Presumably he had visions of his precious film being delayed, so he had me whipped off to hospital for a complete check-up—heart beat, blood pressure, the works. You would have thought I was the Crown Jewels, the way he fussed! I imagine he was also covering himself from the insurance angle. The doctors thought he was making a big fuss about nothing, but he insisted I be given a thorough overhaul. Then he arranged an ambulance and a private nurse, though God knows what she'll find to do. I can hobble about quite happily on my own.' He laughed. 'Apparently all I need is a couple of days' rest, and I'll be back on my feet again. Then I'll be at the disco with you, instead of that bloody Chuck.'

There was a bite in his voice, and Caitlin eyed him warily.

'What happened last night?'

'Don't worry. We didn't come to blows. I was more concerned about straightening everything out with you than fighting him. I told him straight that if he dared to come near you again I'd flatten him.' He tapped his index finger reprovingly on her chin. 'But you can nardly blame the guy for fancying a girl who dances half naked in front of him.

'I wasn't half naked,' she retaliated, denying the knowledge that her dress and her behaviour had been deliberately provocative. 'In any case, what I choose to wear is my own business.'

'You were damn lucky you weren't raped, flaunting yourself like some good-time girl,' he rasped.

Temper glittered in her eyes. 'I'll be a good-time girl if I wish!'

She had no idea why she was arguing with him, when all she wanted was to be held tight in the circle of his arms. Bryce rubbed her chin.

'You're not the good-time girl type, Cait. You're the faithful kind. You belong to me and always will,' he warned softly. 'I'm damned if I'll allow you to tease other men like that.'

A spark of feminine independence burst alight. 'I'm not yours.'

'You are.' His voice was low and certain. 'You gave yourself to me. I'm your first lover and I intend to be your last.'

'The grand old masculine double standard,' she taunted. 'You've had plenty of love affairs, why do you imagine you have the right to limit me to one?'

The question was academic. She knew she would never love anyone else, but she refused to be claimed so easily.

'Because you're going to marry me, that's why.'

Her eyes widened. 'You don't believe in marriage.' Her fury was spent, and now she was suspicious. 'You told me that in the very first interview. You said you didn't believe in restricting yourself to one woman. Why should you change now?'

A black brow arched. 'Did I say that, or did Slattery?'

Caitlin flushed, dropping her eyes from his.

'I love you very much, my darling.' His voice was gently assuring. Her chin lifted.

'Then why did you turn me away from the film set? You could have countermanded Frank's instructions.' She blinked away a rush of unshed tears, remembering the humiliation.

'They were *my* instructions.' He drew an aimless pattern on the sheet with his finger, then looked up. 'I told Frank to make sure you didn't come on set. To be honest I never thought there was a chance you would try, but I had to play safe. I didn't want you to see me as Slattery.' The side of his mouth twisted.

'But why not? What difference does it make?' she asked with a frown.

The finger moved haphazardly. 'None, I hope, but I couldn't be certain. You didn't seem very clear about who was the real me.' He shot her a glance. 'When I'm acting I tend to absorb the character. It's different when I'm in public. Then I turn on and off the "mental swagger" as you call it. The transition is easy, it's a shallow thing. But when I spend hours dressed in Slattery's clothes, speaking his words, it becomes harder suddenly to eliminate him. Remnants of his style tend to linger for a while. I was terrified that if you saw me when I was acting you might start having doubts again about our relationship.' He sighed. 'I couldn't bear to lose you, Cait.'

She bent forward and slipped an arm around his neck, her lashes fluttering over his cheek.

'I know who you are, Bryce, and I love you. I don't give a damn about Slattery.'

'And you'll marry me?' His question was gruff.

'If you're sure that's what you want,' she murmured, nestling against him.

'Of course I'm sure. I've spent all my life looking for a girl like you, and now that I've found you I have no intention of allowing you to escape.'

He kissed her, gently at first, but then his mouth parted on hers and inexorably they found themselves gasping as the undertow of desire pulled at them.

'Let's make love,' he muttered, as his fingers explored the curves beneath the thin cotton voile.

'What about your ankle?' she asked against the smooth skin of his shoulder.

'To hell with my ankle!'

'Wait a minute.' Caitlin sat up. 'Tell me something.'

He sighed impatiently. 'What?'

'Why did you give me that fake interview the first time we met?'

He gave a sheepish grin. 'I was in the middle of what I suppose the newspapers might call an "identity crisis", he confessed. 'It was as though Slattery had taken over my life, and I was finding it difficult to decide where he ended and I began. To make matters worse, the evening before you interviewed me I was entertaining an actress and she called me Slattery, purely by mistake, at a rather intense moment.' He stroked the back of Caitlin's hand. 'It shattered my ego. I thought that if she, as a member of the acting profession, was confused by the image, then there wasn't much hope left. I wanted to walk away from fame, from Slattery, from everything and find myself again. Then you appeared, all sweetness and light, and you called me Slattery, too.' He raised a hand in a vague gesture and let it fall back on the sheet. 'Something snapped inside me. I needed revenge, but in a strange way it was revenge on Slattery. It really had nothing to do with you. At first I was delighted when I saw you scribbling down everything so earnestly, but then I began to have cold feet. That's why I suggested you contact my agent. Even then I thought you'd twig on to my deception the minute you sat down and considered your notes.'

'But I didn't.' Caitlin tried to ignore the musky fragrance of his skin which was sending messages of desire throbbing in her veins.

'I miscalculated,' he admitted. 'I didn't realise that you were so naïve and trusting.' Gently he tugged at her earlobe. 'You've matured beautifully since then.'

'Like rotten cheese or old Fords?' She arched a teasing brow.

'Like a woman with a classical beauty which will last for ever,' he said firmly. 'When we met in Derbyshire you took my breath away. You were special. I could hardly keep my hands off you, as you probably noticed.' They shared a grin. 'But I didn't quite trust you.'

'I was planning to write an exposé on the overstuffed

Bryce Cameron,' she confessed.

'Thanks,' he said drily. 'But by that time I had clarified my position with Slattery. He had ceased to overlap. I had the character firmly in its place. I was well aware when I was me, and when I was him.' Mischief danced in his eyes. 'But you weren't sure, were you?'

She pouted. 'No.'

He laughed. 'I could see you swinging between us, and it made me wary. Somehow you weren't as straightforward as the other women I'd known. There was a gleam in your eye that told me you fancied me, but you were damned if you would admit it, even to yourself.'

'I wasn't prepared to become yet another Slattery conquest.'

He put an arm around her shoulders, pulling her close. 'You're not, my darling. I've never felt about anyone as I feel about you.'

His hand moved across her ribcage.

'But why didn't you contact me when I returned to London?' she asked, determined to understand all the facts before she surrendered herself to the desire warming her blood.

Reluctantly he sighed and his hand stilled. 'I did try to get in touch when you first vanished,' he explained. 'But at the time there was a great deal of pressure from my agent, the lawyers, and the press about my future plans. I rang your number whenever I had a free moment, but the damn phone was always engaged. I couldn't work up the impetus to write, because I didn't know what I could say. It was a confusing time. I was being forced into snap decisions which I knew would alter my life irrevocably, and you were an added complication.' He gave a bleak laugh. 'When the clamour eased off I began to wonder exactly what it was I wanted from you. I sensed that it had to be all or nothing. I also felt guilty about my behaviour towards you at the fête, and uneasy because you were due to be married. I didn't know if I had the right to intrude on your life any further.' His hand travelled along her arm to her shoulder. 'I could hardly destroy your future marriage and offer nothing in return.'

'So why did you arrange with Alison for me to come out here?' Caitlin asked, puzzled. 'You didn't know Matthew and I had split up.'

'I couldn't stop myself. I was desperate to see you again. I had reached the stage where I couldn't sleep at nights for thinking about you, and I was going silently crazy.' His lip twitched at the wry admission. 'When I quizzed Alison about your relationship with Matthew she denied any knowledge of marriage plans, so I decided to take a chance. I convinced myself that because I wanted you so much, you might feel the same.'

He curled a hand in her hair and pulled the scarf from her ponytail, watching as the curls tumbled on to her shoulders. Then his fingers moved to the shoestring strap on one shoulder. Caitlin tried to stem the mounting excitement of his touch, but without success.

'I felt somewhat in awe of the situation because you were a virgin,' he mumbled, leaning forward to kiss the side of her mouth.

'How did you know?'

He raised his head. 'You were different from the other girls. They were so . . .' He paused. 'So damned easy. The minute I smiled their way, they started undressing. To them making love was a casual gesture. They gave themselves casually, and I suppose I took in the same manner.' He frowned at the admission. 'But you weren't like that. I'd never slept with a virgin before, and I had no intention of making love to you and then walking away. Unfortunately, I was still troubled by the idea that you'd betrayed me to the press.'

'But I didn't!' Her face flushed with indignation.

'I know that now,' he smiled, rubbing his nose against hers. 'Frank confessed all.'

'Frank?'

'That's what the argument was about before I made my death defying leap from the step,' he chuckled. 'One of the crew let it slip just how bloody unpleasant Frank had been towards you, and I tackled him about it. There was no reason for his attitude. He could have politely explained and asked you to leave.' His fingers toyed with the strap. 'One thing led to another and we ended up yelling at each other. Our relationship has always been tense. He resents me because he thinks Eleanor and I were lovers.'

Her brow puckered. 'And were you?'

He shook his head and smiled. 'Eleanor is like an older sister. She helped me get started in the early days, but it's always been strictly platonic. Frank doesn't believe that. He's been in love with her for years, but she always keeps him at arm's length, and for some reason he blames me.' He glanced obliquely at her. 'Everyone imagines I've had a riproaring love life, but believe me, it hasn't been anywhere near as prolific as the media make out.'

'Your alter ego was the culprit?' Her eyes sparkled.

He winked. 'Blame Slattery, the dream hero.' His expression became serious. 'While Frank and I were shouting at each other he blurted out how pleased he was that he had released the premature news of my departure. He said he was delighted to see how much trouble he'd caused me. Once he'd spoken, he shut up. He could see from the look on my face just how livid I was.' Bryce rubbed his scar in agitation. 'I had talked over the idea of terminating my contract with Eleanor, and apparently she had let the odd word slip and Frank had pounced on it and realised my intentions.'

'But why should he leak the information?'

'Partly to satisfy his grievance over Eleanor, and partly because he saw it as extra publicity for the film—last chance to see Slattery, that angle.'

'Have you sorted out your contract now?' Caitlin asked, nestling in the crook of his arm.

'Yes. The lawyers finally worked out a deal which keeps everyone happy. It won't go to court. Financially I'm slightly worse off, but I shall recover.'

He untied the strap on her shoulder, exposing one full breast. Caitlin closed her eyes and sighed as his hand moved upwards to possess it.

'Frank and I finally calmed down,' he said. 'We've patched up our quarrel. He apologises for all the trouble he's caused and sends his congratulations on our marriage.'

Her hazel eyes widened. 'You told him! But you hadn't asked me. Suppose I'd refused?'

With slow deliberation he began to kiss her temples, her nose, her chin, her throat. 'I knew after we'd made love that you would never be able to resist me again,' he murmured throatily, bending his head as he transferred his attentions to her naked shoulders.

'Pure Slattery!' Caitlin teased.

His fingers tugged at the second bow on her shoulder.

'Most women would be delighted to marry a millionaire detective,' he taunted softly.

'Not me.' Her body arched, submitting to the caress of his hands.

His voice was husky. 'You'd settle for a motor mechanic?'

'Only if he's called Bryce Cameron,' she conceded.

And then there was silence.

THE MUSIC OF MOZART

When Caitlin interviews Bryce, she discovers that one of his favorite pastimes is listening to the music of Mozart, a composer considered by many to be the greatest musical genius of all time.

Wolfgang Amadeus Mozart was born in 1756 in Salzburg, Austria. His father, Leopold, a well-known violinist and composer, taught his son how to play harpsichord at a very early age, and young Mozart performed his first piano recital when he was only three. By the time he was five, Mozart was composing music, and when he was six, his father took him to Munich and Vienna on his first concert tour. Soon Mozart was being commissioned by European royalty, including the Empress Maria Theresa of Austria, to write music for state weddings and church ceremonies.

In those days, composers earned their keep by working in the households of noblemen or wealthy clergymen. Mozart's patron for many years was the archbishop of Salzburg. But the archbishop was a spiteful and jealous man, refusing to allow Mozart to play for anyone else and forcing him to eat with the servants. Finally, in 1781, the archbishop was unspeakably rude to Mozart in public, and consequently the young musician resigned and moved to Vienna.

There, he met and fell in love with Constanze Weber, whom he married. But without a patron Mozart had terrible financial problems and fell heavily into debt. In 1791, at the age of thirty-five, he became seriously ill and died, and was given only a pauper's burial.

Yet despite his brief life, Mozart left a magnificent legacy for future generations—hundreds of pieces of music, from brilliant symphonies to such famous operas as *The Marriage of Figaro* and *The Magic Flute*. Eminent music scholars have said that, with Mozart, European music reached its highest point of perfection.

ROBERTA LEIGH
Collector's Edition

A specially designed collection of six exciting love stories by one of the world's favorite romance writers—Roberta Leigh, author of more than 60 bestselling novels!

Available in August wherever paperback books are sold, or available through Harlequin Reader Service. Simply complete and mail the coupon below.

Harlequin Reader Service

In the U.S.   In Canada
P.O. Box 52040   649 Ontario Street
Phoenix, AZ 85072-9988   Stratford, Ontario N5A 6W2

Please send me the following editions of the Harlequin Roberta Leigh Collector's Editions. I am enclosing my check or money order for $1.95 for each copy ordered, plus 75¢ to cover postage and handling.

☐ 1   ☐ 2   ☐ 3   ☐ 4   ☐ 5   ☐ 6

Number of books checked_____ @ $1.95 each = $_____
N.Y. state and Ariz. residents add appropriate sales tax $_____
Postage and handling $____.75____
                                               TOTAL $_____

I enclose_____

(Please send check or money order. We cannot be responsible for cash sent through the mail.) Price subject to change without notice.

NAME_____
                        (Please Print)
ADDRESS_____APT. NO._____
CITY_____
STATE/PROV._____ZIP/POSTAL CODE_____

Offer expires December 31, 1983.   30656000000

RL-A

What romance fans say about Harlequin...

"...scintillating, heartwarming...
a very important, integral part of mass-
market literature."
—J.G.,* San Antonio, Texas

"...it is a pleasure to escape behind a
Harlequin and go on a trip to a faraway
country."
—B.J.M., Flint, Michigan

"Their wonderfully depicted settings make
each and every one a joy to read."
—H.B., Jonesboro, Arkansas

*Names available on request.